NEW DIRECTIONS 43

For Else Albrecht-Carrié

New Directions in Prose and Poetry 43

Edited by J. Laughlin

with Peter Glassgold and Frederick R. Martin

 A New Directions Book

ACKNOWLEDGMENTS
Grateful acknowledgment is made to the editors and publishers of books and magazines in which some of the selections in this volume first appeared: for Homero Aridjis, *Exaltation of Light,* Boa Editions (English translation, Copyright © 1981 by Eliot Weinberger); for Mario Cesariny, *The Journal of The American Portuguese Society* (Copyright © 1978 by The American Portuguese Society, Inc.); for Antonio Cisneros, *Caliban, Lettera;* for Joan Retallack, *Ambit, The Massachusetts Review;* for Eliot Weinberger, *Zero* (Copyright © 1981 by Zero Press). Guillevic's "Six Poems" appear in translation with the permission of Editions Gallimard, Paris. "Elegies," "When," and "Encounter" were published in *Etier* (© Editions Gallimard, 1979), "The Charnel Houses" and "Portraits" in *Terraqué* (© Editions Gallimard, 1942), and "Magnificat" in *La Nouvelle Revue Français* (May 1977).

Manufactured in the United States of America
First published clothbound (ISBN: 0–8112–0811–7) and as New Directions Paperbook 524 (ISBN: 0–8112–0812–5) in 1981
Published simultaneously in Canada by George J. McLeod, Ltd., Toronto

New Directions Books are published for James Laughlin
by New Directions Publishing Corporation,
80 Eighth Avenue, New York 10011

CONTENTS

Homero Aridjis
    Eleven Poems   10

Edwin Brock
    Two Poems   63

Mario Cesariny
    Five Poems   160

Antonio Cisneros
    Four Poems   147

Ruth Domino
    Four Poems   128

Robin Gajdusek
    Six Poems   72

Guillevic
    Six Poems   88

Russell Haley
    The Palace of Kandahar   47

Rüdiger Kremer
    The Grasslandsman   17

Lawrence Millman
    Origins   134

Ursule Molinaro
     A Diet of Worms   78

Alain Nadaud
     Interview with Samuel Astonguet   115

António Osório
     Five Poems   164

Justo Jorge Padrón
     Six Poems   140

Boško Petrović
     Three Poems   180

James Purdy
     What Is It, Zach?   171

Giovanni Raboni
     The Coldest Year of Grace   132

Michael Reck
     Seven Poems   65

Joan Retallack
     Four Poems   43

Geoffrey Rips
     Stray Dogs   154

Anne Waldman
     Putting Makeup on Empty Space   38

Eliot Weinberger
     Cello Solo   1

Notes on Contributors   183

CELLO SOLO

ELIOT WEINBERGER

For Jonathan Griffen

Like many others I've examined
The world in a drop of pond
And the archaeology of a leaf
The revolutions of history
The repetitions of myth
The intricate finity of a song of words
And the small comforts in the cracks of silence
The telephone's antiphony Miscalled speech
The daily tales of government cruelty
Art dead in execution
And the executions of the luckless just
The end of the edible End of the respirable
The end of the aromatic
There are storms in the brain that wash out the mind
On summer nights I peer at ghostly Saturn

 •

And you must say no if asked
If the electron retains the same place
You must say no
If its position changes with time

1

If in motion   If at rest   Say no
On summer nights there is a ring around the city
Citizens pale in the glow to fiddle knobs
Each night no end to that far world
Luxury & disaster
I sit in the heat watching
The image of man flicker
Ghosts in the living rooms   They are
As you try to learn what they are

     •

Out of old tales you hope
To open the sky
But no the sky never opens
Particles interact
Filmed & played forward or back
Are the same   The same
Unbearably infinite
The vacuum among & within the motes
A finity beyond the mind
With time dead you kill time
Examining the execution of speech
Till golden morpheme bringeth sleep
Yes there was a message in the bottle
But the bottle dissolved
Stuck in a slick-nacred sea

     •

Dioxin-dumped, the brain, the ocean floor
What embryonic monsters   The canisters
The world keeps to dredge in sleep
No crackle in the waves no hiss
The ghosts of plankton never linger
What living manta hover ever
In the taste of sludge
So a leaf falls
The same leaf falls

The same leaf falls again
& lost in the riddle who sees
The disappearance of the trees

    •

A fish dies   Dies & rises to meet the leaf
Her eyes on her release
On the city floor the holothurians
Eat mud   Excrete mud   Eat mud
To get a little taste
The phone rings
There is a lightning bolt
Spiders cross the brickwork meaning rain
A silence at the other end
And no bird sings   It must be rain
Yet only yesterday & the day before
Yes the day before that

    •

It was more visible in everything than in nothing
It is an archaeology of dreams
Skull stuck in the cliffside
A guide points
Here is a world to extrapolate
A blank globe
The unexcavated mind   But what
Would a mud-brain say but no
The phone again
Crackling like a living sea
Drowned voices wake us till we are human
& nightmares begin
As the old dreams rise to the present tense

    •

Yes there is a sky above
I sit in the downdraft

In the pentecostal breeze
Waiting for sound to echo back
To a static brain
Catkins rustle in the lake's seiche
Yes then you were there
     & the wind turned back the conflagration
Then there
     the tigers suddenly fled
     cubs on their backs
     across the Yellow River
He replied:
     It was all pure chance
And the annalists were instructed to record
His irrelevancy

   •

There is a message
Long-dancing in the holy spirals
We are what we are   Who can learn it
Relay stations   Chickens
In existence that the egg
May make another egg
Irrelevancy's a badge of honor
Switch off the lights
The airwaves are full of voices

   •

Not how or why but that
It is—It is
Star-shaped, the seeds in the wind
The wash and flush of solar wind
Squiggles & dots: we, us, our
Masses of particles & waves brushing up
Against the other
             The static sparks
& vanishes as we pass by

Not poetry: every day dying
From lack of friction

•

That rock is that which man is not
But the object is to become the rock
There is a face in the rock-face
Look there in the lichen
On another face: the face
In stained pavement: the face of rain:
The mob-face: the faces of ants pouring out from the rock
Look there in the lichen
                    Said Pir of Herat
& do not be surprised by sorrow
After all this is only the world

•

Like the pillar in the mind of God
Like the antenna in the spine of man
Like the last standing cedar
Receive her
They flock about like bats
They dome her head like stars
They speak in shapes
Saying less than they intend
There at the bend of the willow
In pa ra dise In pa ra dise
In paradise

•

I sit in the heat
In the windless flush of particles to watch
The wash of the particular world
The crack of light through the fingers
The light points from my fingertips

The clawed hands that type
Spider on a leaf meaning rain
Though there's not a spider
Few leaves, no rain   Only
A ball of air the hand cups
And cannot lift
It is a heap of bones
It is a heap of carved stones
The workmen are hooded
Archaeologists
Hammers in each hand cracking

.

In paradise a crow speaks
When he cannot say   All's well
He says all will be well
But what does a crow know of ill befallen
In paradise the crows forget the answers
Or what doesn't he
In paradise the kids eat Kronos
Place erases into space
& space is the star-shaped seed
Lifting over the pentecostal flames
It is not a sack   It is not a cell
Lux my fair crow   In paradise
There are no scarecrows
In paradise we forget the question
& leave town

.

Not cruelty, organized or random
Not the villagers digging grubs from cracked land
Not the alley, not the pogrom
Not Kent State, not 1919
(coffins stacking on the pier)
Not the rain of chemical fire
The canisters of nerve gas

The daily tales of world's end
Not even the mad brains
Here on a murky floor of the world
Barely hidden in the passers-by
But terror there is terror
When the fingers strike the letters
s, k, and y

·

The skull is a shanty in old Chinatown
The skull is a shanty
                    & there's no one around
My eyes are the windows of old shantytown
My eyes are the windows
                    when the shades are down
But the shades are out in old Chinatown
And the shades sing a chantey
When the shanties are empty
And you can't hear the sound
Wind sings through the sockets in old Chinatown
Skull   Eye   Shade   Wind   Sound

·

Insofar as it refers to reality
It is not certain
Insofar as it is certain
It refers not to reality
There is no face on the rock-face
There is only a face
                    watching the rock
& when you cannot face that face
Something will rush to meet you

·

The star collapses   matter grows dense
& so grows the gravity

Light waves stretching out   trapped
Till starlight disappear though the thing remain
Charted by its absence   by light's lack behind
On summer nights bricks fall from the facades
There is a manhole cover   A manta
Hovering in the oily haze of an empty street
And the light turns green and you cannot move
The light turns green
And you can't move forward
There is nothing across the crossroads
There is nothing there is nothing
There is nothing there
A swarm of shades tangle in the heat
Without symbols   Without self
Their eyes as though the moon shone elsewhere
Without a sound

.

In the great cold hall
Two women   Rocking
Their faces covered with blood
Blood rains on the windows
Smearing the glass
And the drowned man, the deaf & dumb
The luckless just just stand there
Here in my brain waiting for us
To come in from the storm

.

And the luckless just just stand there
It is not the terror of the sky
That giant sky   That sky
Whose points of fire we connect
To write our daily tales of other worlds
Of chemical life   Gaseous life
Of earths that are the mirror of this earth
It is not that terror that breaks the I

But the fresh report of disaster
There is an antenna in the spine of man
& who can bear
To bear that news within

.

To switch it off to hear intricity
To crawl eyeless on the city floor
To switch it off
& sink in stars' harmonia
The patterns of particle & molecule
The long-dancing message
That sings in the spirals
That will sing in spite
To switch it off & live in static
Yes this hand is a retreat
The airwaves are full of voices
Shades sing in the alley
Their songs smear the window
The repetition of history
The tale of blood running
Through the brain & through the street
Like many others
I try to live within this shape

ELEVEN POEMS

HOMERO ARIDJIS

Translated from the Spanish by Eliot Weinberger

TEZCATLIPOCA

1
that shadow
that clash
that eye passing through the rocks
that dry branch on the green tree
that thorn in a girl's breast
that disillusion (dissolution) in the things of man
that dog's rage of man
that solitude in the spoon   in the walls
that air
that affliction
that mirror
where all things must vanish

2
that clenched fist
that flattened spider
that dog's old eyes
that fang that rips things

that invisibility things
move toward (without moving)
that mange on the donkey's back
and in the mouth of man
that endless war
that pain
that rage
knows everything
can do everything
is everywhere
like darkness
like the mind

BURN THE BOATS

Burn the boats
that the old shadows
will not follow us
to the new land

that those who travel with me
will not think it possible
to return to what they were
in the lost country

that we find
only the sea at our backs
and the unknown before us

that we walk without fear
through the ashes
into the here and now

THERE ARE BIRDS IN THIS LAND

(Fr. Bernardino de Sahagún)

There are birds in this land
there is song from the green to the dry
there is a tree of many names
there is mixed mud and straw
there is a rock in the night
like a firefly that doesn't move
there is a twittering of dust on the plains
there is a river that climbs a mountain
with a murmur that grows thin
there is man   there is light
there are birds in this land

DREAM IN TENOCHTITLAN

1
All night
I crossed the canal
between white houses
oars in the water cut
the hushed green of the willows
and the shadows of the temples swirled
from the other side of the canal
you came in a yellow boat
your face painted red
and for a moment our boats
met beneath the blue bridge
and then I couldn't follow
        your eyes watching me
        rays of light
        fixed in my heart

2
In the air your eyes left
blue birds
and your body left
luminous bodies in its wake
around you everything
became calm
people passing in the street
entered each other without leaving themselves
     I traveled through your transparent head
     I raised your weightless hands
     I drank light from your breast
     I

a black rooster woke us

POPOCATÉPETL

The mountain floats over time
like crystallized thought

white over the valley
the days don't seem to move it

not the days that made it
nor those
that will bring it down

ZAPATA

He did not die
riddled with bullets
at the door of the hacienda

that day in April
when the soldiers
at the bugle's
last note
twice emptied
their rifles

those who saw him say
he withstood the bullets
men and time
and on a white horse
at full gallop
rode into death unharmed

BARBERSHOP

Sunday morning
the peasants
solemnly enter the barbershop
to wait their turn
and leave   after a while
hat in hand
looking
as though a meadow
had been cleared
from their heads

LETTER FROM MEXICO

Invisible ancestors
walk with us
through these back streets

car-noises
the stares of children
young girls' bodies
cross through them

Weightless   vague
we travel through them
at doorways that no longer are
on bridges that are empty

while with the sun on our faces
we too
move toward transparency

THIS IS ALTAMIRANO HILL

This is Altamirano Hill
I have crossed its forest
watched its oak acacia and beech
have stepped on their roots
tugged at their leaves
but there is no tree
lovelier than your body

THE HILL OF THE STAR

I've come too late
to see the gods
fly over these hills

but between the gray peaks
of this burnt hill

I find the stones
of a visible god
smashed to bits

MEXICO CITY

Streets of cement
that go
where the river ran

lamp posts
in place
of the ancient trees

bodies cross through
the ancestral bodies
who called this river *atoyatl*
and this tree *teocotl*

passages replace passages
ghosts replace ghosts
words replace words

THE GRASSLANDSMAN

RÜDIGER KREMER

Translated from the German by Breon Mitchell

Potocki, Jan Count: *Polish scholar and poet, b. March 8, 1761 in Pikow—d. December 2, 1815 in Uladowka (suicide). Studied mathematics, lived in Warsaw, London, Paris, and Spain and Morocco; supported the French Revolution and undertook extensive journies, as far as China, as Privy Councilor to Czar Alexander of Russia. Historian and antiquarian, founder of Slavic archaeology, conversant with Oriental languages. His historical and geographical publications in French are still valuable source books today. His one work of fiction, a philosophical framed-tale with a complicated and multilayered plot, filled with elements of fantasy, is entitled* The Saragossa Manuscript.

The radio play "The Grasslandsman" depicts the final moments of Jan Potocki's life. The author uses the classical master-servant relationship, in an ironically disrupted form, in order to create a dialogue between two men of approximately the same age, but radically different experiences and worldviews. Potocki recalls his life, a life full of contradiction and failure, hope and despair. He has failed not only as a man of the Enlightenment and the Revolution but also as a thinker and scientist. The social reforms which he has introduced on his estate, left completely to the law of the most powerful, have led to a situation of chaos. He has therefore withdrawn into the total isolation of his inner world and is writing a long and powerful fantasy novel, a work which totally exhausts

him. At the same time he has been patiently and steadily filing
away at a silver ball, with which he intends to kill himself upon
the completion of his novel. This task, as long as it lasts, gives him
the strength to continue living and writing. The completion of both
the manuscript and the bullet occur on the same day.

The radio play is based on the facts of Potocki's life but deals
with them at the author's discretion to create relationships to other
biographies.—B. R.

Characters: Jan Potocki
Jerzy Luczak

THE DIALOG IS ACCOMPANIED BY THE LOW SOUND OF
A FILE WITH WHICH P. IS SMOOTHING A SILVER BALL
INTENDED AS A BULLET. See indications below.

P.: I am that I am. You'll see! I've got more power over you
than you do over me—if not you'll have to hurry to prove me
wrong, old friend. I've asked you often enough to show me your
power . . . my God, how many times have I begged you to strike
me down as I would slap a fly with a quick movement of my hand.
Did you ever bother to grant my request?—You've let me live till
I'm exhausted. Now it's over! Do you understand? I've gone
against you—for some time now I've ceased to concede that you
have any right over me. Now I'll live and die on my own. I'm
getting rid of you. You didn't strike me down so now I'll strike you
down. There's no spot in all the universe in which we two can live
beside each other—not any longer. You've had every chance but
you've not used one to explain yourself . . . and me. Now I have
my own genealogy, and you can't interrupt me or it any more: a
May beetle fell into the river, was snapped up by a trout, which
was swallowed by a pike. A fisherman caught the pike and brought
it to the table of the Count. Strengthened by his fish dinner, the
Count was filled with lust and bedded my mother. Thus did he
conceive me, his heir, Count Jan von Potocki. But I am actually
the son of a May beetle—and it is to these facts alone that I may

lay the blame for my lifelong inability to dream of anything but flies. There you have the story of my origin, and I say to you again:

I am that I am. I was that I was. I will be that I will be. In the great city of Paris and the ancient city of Urumchi. In Saragossa too, and here. Back then, today, later. Preferably later. And in another world. Mountainless, I would like most of all to walk eternally on the grassy plains toward the horizon. In Mongolia, in Outer Mongolia. Yes, God of the Christians, Jehovah, Allah, Brahma, Manitou . . . Great Spirit . . . wake me once more in a sea of grass, when you wish to resurrect me. Only as bird may you place me in the mountains, only as a bird, as an eagle, a hawk, as a falcon—if need be even as a jackdaw. No other kinds please. After all I've seen the world and know what I'm talking about. Would you like to be a wren or a red-throated robin? Only with my throat slit, I tell you, only with my throat slit. And that's excluded—I've seen too many slit throats in my lifetime.

I speak to you now as an equal: You are that you are and I am that I am, God of the Christians, you have no hold on me. You think I'm one of them? I admit, there were times when I wished I were a humble Christian, a monk, a hermit, a shadow of your image. But if you exist, you've read all my books, including this one here. Admit it, I've disproved you and I spurn you. And if, contrary to all of science, you did exist, it would prove nothing. On the contrary, it would make you ridiculous. I could believe in a thousand gods, but not in you, the single one. Look!

VIGOROUS FILING

You can't do anything to me. I'll determine the course of everything myself—I deny you the slightest say: so no slit throats, no robin redbreasts. (*Giggles*) After all, I am, whether I like it or not, a nobleman. A count, a man of the world, a man of science and a poet. I won't compare your work with mine—but one thing is certain: I prefer my own. You play only one part in it. The role that I have set aside for you—scoundrel, blockhead, senile old fool, moralist, murderer—a coward in the face of death. If you at least would die! Can't you, or won't you? You've been dead for a long time you know, why won't you give up the ghost? We disproved you long ago. Galileo, Keppler, Newton, Rousseau, Voltaire, and I—oh yes, admittedly Voltaire finally crawled to the cross—but I could name others who didn't crawl to the cross—and I'll tell you one thing: there are getting to be more and more of us . . .

Plainsmen, walking through the grass toward the horizon. You don't have a chance against us, plainsmen, we're not frightened by death. We've put ourselves in your place, at least since 1789 you've been forced to share things, and your share of the world is growing steadily smaller—it's a good thing we destroyed the myths that surrounded you. Now we are the masters of the world—but we will pass it on to all those who live upon it. Soon there will be no more master and mistress—no masters and no mastered. Whoever draws breath shall be master—of himself. I know, you don't believe in that, but I want to believe in it. Yes, I want to believe it, and you'll see, that I . . .

THERE IS A KNOCK AT THE DOOR

Stay here, old friend, I'm not quite finished yet. (*Loudly*) Yes, come in . . .

THE DOOR IS OPENED AND CLOSED

L.: Master, if I may be permitted . . .
P.: Don't call me master!
L.: No master, most humbly . . .
P.: Don't call me master and certainly not most humbly!
L.: Your excellency . . .
P.: Devil take it, call me by my name!
L.: Count Potocki . . .
P.: Potocki, just Potocki, Citizen Potocki.
L.: Your excellency, Count . . .
P.: Citizen!
L.: Citizen von Potocki.
P.: Citizen Potocki—without the von—simply Potocki.
L.: Citizen Potocki, I wish to report to the Count that the horse has been saddled and awaits your excellency in the courtyard.
P.: (*Laughs*)

L.: . . . as your excellency ordered.

P.: Stand up properly . . . straighter . . . and hands at your side . . . where are your white gloves?

L.: Your grace . . .

P.: . . . and why aren't your shoes Viennesed?

L.: Count . . .

P.: Your uniform is threadbare!

L.: Master, it's been a long time since we had any white gloves, and all the uniforms are threadbare—mine is practically still new!

P.: Bow your head! . . . That's right . . . Humility, my old friend! Tell me what your name is!

L.: Permit me, excellency—your excellency . . .

P.: Your name!

L.: Master . . .

P.: Your name . . . at least tell me your name!

L.: Luczak, master, you must know me.

P.: Spell it!

L.: *Luczak*, master, l, U, c, z, A, K.

P.: No, I don't know it. How were you baptized?

L.: Master, I don't understand . . .

P.: I want to know what name you were given at baptism!

L.: Jerzy.

P.: Jerzy?—that's all, just Jerzy?

L.: Yes, master, Jerzy Luczak, just Jerzy Luczak, nothing more.

P.: Do you know my name?

L.: Of course, your excellency.

P.: Leave out all my titles and call me by my name!

L.: Count, excellency . . . Jan Count von Potocki, Doctor of Philosophy, Doctor of . . .

P.: Jerzy Luczak . . .

E.: Your grace?

P.: Shut up! Leave out all the titles and doctorates and tell me what you call me when you're with your friends, working in the stables.

L.: Master . . .

P.: If you try to wriggle out of it, I'll floor you! Man, do you want to feel the fist of your master?

L.: I would be sorry to let myself in for a beating, master.

p.: Well, then?

l.: We call your excellency the Wastrel.

––––––––

p.: Not bad. Jan Potocki, the Wastrel, Citizen Jan Count von Potocki, the Wastrel—you've made an apt choice. It almost sounds poetic. —How did you think of it?

l.: Your grace, we didn't mean to . . .

p.: What are you supposed to call me?

l.: Citizen . . . Citizen Potocki, I . . . I guess . . . because everything is wasting away here—everything, the castle, the estate, the fields, the animals, we're wasting away—and in the middle of it all, you're wasting away in your library. Everything has been wasting away, going from bad to worse steadily for years, and no one is doing anything to put a stop to it. If only the old Count, your blessed father, had lived to see how things have . . .

p.: Don't speak to me about my father, the fisheater.

l.: Your excellency—I mean Citizen Potocki—the servants need a strong hand again, an iron fist with a steel rod. No one does a decent day's work any more, your manager manages things into his own pocket as best he can, the peasants steal the crops from the fields and the cattle from the meadow. The steward wears your best clothes and your own boots. He sleeps with all the young women and the chambermaids. He runs the house as if he were the master—everyone is free to do as he wishes without fear of punishment. Master, re-establish justice! Let those who are lazy be publicly flogged, hang the cattle thieves, castrate the rapists . . .

p.: Quiet, Luczak . . . and relax. I know that not all things are going well on the estate. But I have neither the desire nor the time to worry about your affairs. If the uniforms are ragged, then throw them away and put on ordinary clothes. If you live without justice, then make the laws under which you wish to live, work it out among yourselves. Pour me a drink from the bottle there!

SOUNDS OF POURING, ETC.

Potato schnapps—disgusting. Where's the plum brandy gone to?

l.: The plum trees have been cut down for firewood . . . and the apple trees and pear trees too.

p.: All right, forget it! Potato schnapps is better than nothing. (*Laughing*) And it's really been a while since we've had wine from Bordeaux . . . Ah, those were the days, wandering like vagabonds through France. Days like pearly dewdrops on spider webs. And when the sunny days began to fade, we drowned the cold October nights in wine. The Gironde, the beautiful Gironde . . . do you remember the Girondists?

l.: No, master, I was never in France.

p.: I don't mean in France, Luczak. Come, sit down . . . no, not there on the stool, sit here beside me in the armchair . . . remember the day I came back from France—back then, when my father, the old Count von Potocki had died, I had you all gather in the courtyard of the castle and spoke to you about the French Revolution from up on the steps. The old man was scarcely in his grave, and I was giving you your freedom, releasing you from a thousand years of bondage.

l.: Yes, master, I remember, it was in 1799, one year before the turn of the century.

p.: Could be . . . I still remember, I told you that man is born free, and that the power of one person over another is not a God-given fact but the devilish work of the human brain. Have you ever heard of Danton?

l.: No, master.

p.: All men are equal.

l.: Yes, master, before God—but not on earth.

p.: I told you back then that the oppressed had freed themselves from their oppressors, that the world of master and mistress was breaking apart on earth, that the oppressed were announcing freedom, equality, and brotherhood here and now.

l.: Yes, master, but we didn't understand your speech. Everyone can't be master. Those who are to be served must be able to issue orders, and the peasant needs the whip, the thief needs his punishment, the prisoner his chains, the murderer his noose. Master, everything was arranged before your arrival here, each person had his place . . .

p.: Each person had his hunger, his misery, his pain—his bondage. Look at yourself Luczak—how old are you?

l.: Sixty-four, master.

p.: You were a slave for half a century, now you're a free man—

a free man. You can go where you wish, you can marry whomever you wish, you can . . .

L.: I'm too old to go away and too old to marry.

P.: Pardon me, Luczak, that's not what I meant—I wanted to say that your life has changed fundamentally in these years.

L.: No, master . . .

P.: Once and for all! Never call me master again, call me Potocki, Jan, or the Wastrel—but not master!

L.: All right . . . Jan Potocki.

P.: So your life hasn't changed fundamentally?

L.: I'm still the head of the stables just like always. I haven't changed. But the horses have. They've become shaggy, old, mean-tempered, and lazy. They're never ridden hard, there aren't any more hunts. We need new blood in the studfarm—at least one new stallion and two new mares . . .

P.: It's not a matter of horses, of animals. It's a matter of you, of all of you, of mankind . . . I've made a republic out of the count-dom Uladowka, an island of freedom in a sea of bondage . . . and you talk to me about horses! We're not here to raise horses for hunting with hounds. We . . . I want to create the new man, the free, self-determined, fraternal man.

L.: Jan Potocki, you've turned a blossoming countdom into a starving asylum for the hungry, the worthless, and the sluggards from all over Poland. Mount your horse and ride through the land. They live in caves in the earth, in tents of animalskin, in brush-wood huts, they live in poverty and filth, they nourish themselves by theft, robbery, and murder. Not a head of livestock is safe in the meadow, not a traveler safe on the road, women don't dare leave the house, and men walk about armed with knives, pikes, and axes.

P.: Luczak, the revolution wasn't made in a day. First we learn from our mistakes . . . And isn't it a good thing that we can offer an asylum to the poor, the tormented, and the persecuted? I dreamed of that, back in Paris . . . On my travels in the service of the Czar I pushed forward to the borders of the civilized world. I experienced the arrogance of power. I've seen how those who lived in stone houses rose up against those in cottages, and those in cottages against those in tents, and those in turn against the ones in grass huts, and these against those who dwelled in caves in the earth. Gun against saber, saber against bow and arrow, bow and arrow against stones, stones against fists, fists against upraised hands . . . Jerzy, I've had to stand by and watch while a scientific expedition to the northern border of China came to naught because of questions of protocol. We couldn't talk to one another—Luczak, not even speak—because we round-eyes didn't want to permit the first right of address to the slant-eyes. We had come through ten thousand miles of desert and plain and had been near death by starvation or thirst a dozen times. We had eaten worms, and licked the dew from the grass, just so that we might live until we reached the goal of our mission. I was approaching madness, a feverish bundle of skin and bones, when we arrived at the border. But the officers of the Czar, in their torn uniforms, insisted on taking the first step, on the right to be first to speak. And when the Chinese refused us that right, we withdrew. Honorably of course, and full of pride, back through the deserts and the plains—eating worms and licking up the dew. We arrived decimated in Petersburg to announce war against the rebels. Luczak, believe me, I'm sick of the missionary's role. I cannot and will not concern myself any longer with the woes or well-being of mankind. They'll have to take care of themselves. I offer this land—conquered by my ancestors and steeped in your blood—to you as your home. Share it as brothers according to your needs, don't ask me for orders or decisions. Let me write in peace—me, the Wastrel, that's all I want from you. I just want to be allowed to pursue my work as one among you.

L.: Potocki, you're the master here—even if you don't want to be—the others still regard you as their master. You're not free to decide such matters either—you can't simply cease being the master just because you've taken it into your head to make everyone in your countdom equal.

P.: I don't want to *make* them equal—they are equal. All men are born equal . . .

L.: We are unequal. If you want to make us equal you'll have to order us to be that way and enforce the order with cudgels, whips, and the noose. Among unequals you can't . . .

P.: What do you know about it? Where have you ever been—how far have you been out of Uladowka?

L.: I was in Warsaw—but that was a long time ago.

p.: You were in Warsaw—think of that. I was in Warsaw too, that was a long time ago as well, as a student—and then I was in London, in Switzerland, in Paris, in Spain—in Africa. I've seen oceans and deserts . . . and men.

PAUSE

Jerzy Luczak, you're a Robespierre. You would cut people down for equality. You want to bring about equality with the ax . . .

L.: No, master, pardon me, Jan Potocki, Wastrel, I see the world as it is, built on inequality, bondage, and envy. There are the hungry and the filled, the free and those who serve, and he who lives in hunger and servitude envies the satisfied man his paunch and the free man his life.

p.: Old friend, you are in truth a radical, a Jacobin: behead the satisfied and you'll put an end to hunger, behead the free and you'll put an end to servitude, behead the handsome and no one will be ugly . . . off with their heads! . . . off with their heads! . . .

L.: I believe in the Holy Trinity of God. I would never dream of thinking such a thing, or even expressing it—I only drew out the conclusions of what you were saying. You can't just go up to people and say, from now on you're free, and equal, and I expect you to be brothers. As long as we can remember we've lived differently, you can't change that with three words. I would gladly be your equal, the equal of a count, but I have no desire to be the equal of a peasant, and the peasant has no wish to be equal to the man without a house, and he no doubt has no wish to be equal to the man who stands beneath the gallows. Potocki, you haven't thought things out fully. You're guilty—at least you share in the guilt—of every murder which takes place in Uladowka, of each injustice.

p.: You don't . . . you don't understand what you're saying, can't possibly understand it . . . but that's not your fault, it's the fault of your God, your simple-minded one-track three-part Christian God . . . Just as you came in you interrupted me, I had him caught in my pincers, he didn't know which way to turn—I disproved him, killed him . . .

L.: In the name of the Father, the Son, and the Holy Ghost!

p.: Go ahead and cross yourself, old friend, that will protect you

from the devil but not from human reason. Let's assume for a
moment that God exists—or existed. If so he gave us our reason
too—even that we might turn it against him. .

L.: That is to sin against the Holy Ghost!

P.: Parson's prattle! The cosmos in which you live—from which
you live, is your brain. Jerzy Luczak, I've measured the size of my
head. It is fifty-one centimeters—I have every right to set these
pitiful centimeters against the infinite stars of the universe—to set
my seven liters of blood against the oceans, the world, against the
sun, moon, and stars. For if I cease to think—and it's a simple
scientific fact that I can only think so long as warm blood pulses
through my intact brain—if I cease to think, then the stars are
extinguished, then there is no more world and no more universe—
and certainly no more god of creation. Everything is a fiction of
the brain, and if I destroy my brain I destroy the world, Jerzy
Luczak, once and for all!

L.: And your immortal soul, master—your immortal soul?

P.: A fiction, a figment of my imagination which refuses to come
to terms with the possibility of its own demise. A dark fog, a plain
of death in power, a nonrefuge of knowledge, eternal truth reveals
itself as infinite lies. There are but two possibilities: one gives one-
self up to failure, or one denies it—denial is salvation. Arrogance
is the highest form of humility. Paradox is the world's equation.
Life is death and death is: giving life a sense in the face of all
adversities—look, what do I have here?

L.: A silver ball.

P.: What am I doing with it?

L.: You're filing it down, smaller and smaller.

P.: Yes, smaller and smaller, but only to a certain final size, not
down to dust. Since November of 1805 I've been filing on it—for
weeks and months at a time, I had almost forgotten it. For twelve
years, ever since I began writing my one great and true book about
life, I've been filing away at my death. What you see here, scarcely
the size of the ball of my thumb, was once the size of my fist, a
lion's head of solid silver, the crown of my father's samovar. The
eyes, the mane, the hungry roaring jaws . . . I've filed them all
down to the purest geometrical form. To a sphere. Look, Jerzy, I
place it on the muzzle of my dueling pistol. Only a few more
fractions of a millimeter and it will drop into the barrel . . . now

it still rests on the muzzle, but a few shavings from here, and here and here, and then it will go in smoothly. It will fall into the steel barrel with a ringing click, and turn within: click, click, click . . . I'll roll it about for a moment or so, just to hear the delicate sound, to finally hear what I have only been able to imagine over the years, the silvery ring of my little sphere . . . then rammed home with tow and powder on the pan. You fill your mouth with water . . . or better yet wine, not for its effect, but for the taste in your mouth; but it's been a long time since we've had wine in the house—I should have thought to keep aside one last bottle, a fine Bordeaux, a velvety Pommery, in which to bathe my tongue, to rinse my uvula, to warm nicely my stomach and veins . . . but water achieves the same effect. You fill your mouth with water, lean back your head, place the muzzle of the pistol in your mouth, carefully between the lips, with the barrel angled upward toward the roof of the skull, and press the trigger. The water causes the brain to blow apart, an explosion of the head in all directions—north, south, east and west—as I have traveled the world. A repetition of all my travels, completed in a fraction of a second, all of my experience released into the universe for ever.

I've finished my book. It's to be called "The Saragossa Manuscript." I'm just writing the final sentence . . . and do you know, brother, I wrote the book in French and not in our language; I'd like to have time to write it again in Polish, but I don't have any more time . . . posterity can worry about that. I'm giving it up, Luczak, I'm at the end of my strength . . .

L.: Your excellency, the horse is saddled, you wished to go into the city. There are new public houses—French wine and prostitutes, young girls from Uladowka to whom you have a right, my count. You've just turned fifty-four—I've already borne life ten years longer than you—and it often wasn't easy. You still have a lot to give the world, you've got a head on your shoulders. No one knows more than you do. A scientist and a poet, Jan, Count, Wastrel.

P.: You're lying, or to put it more accurately, I know better than you—I don't have anything else to give to the world. I never had anything to give . . . Are you listening to me?

L.: Yes, master.

P.: You were going to try not to call me master. You could at least learn to do that for me . . .

L.: Yes . . . I won't forget it again.

P.: . . . to call me by my name like a brother.

PAUSE

In Warsaw and London I studied mathematics. I wanted to learn, to know, how the world functioned. To express the world in formulas and solve them—not for me, for everyone. But I didn't discover the world's formula—any more than the alchemists had. In Paris I heard the speeches of the revolution:

PAUSE

Mirabeau, Marat, Danton, Saint-Just, Robespierre. And it seemed as if the scales fell from my eyes. The world-formula had been a child's game. The mysteries were not to be solved, they were to be denied. Science had to push forward from the known into the unknown, farther and farther—but not in order to play numerical games with world-formulas. Neither I nor anyone else could understand the world, only mankind as a whole in the progress of knowledge can . . .

Are you listening to me?

L.: Yes, Jan Potocki, I'm listening to you . . . go on.

P.: All the brains in the world thinking together. What energy and what will power could be set free . . . To conquer fear, and fly, and walk through the grass . . . to be an untrailed grasslandsman free of fear and fly up to the Pleiad, to wing thought with dreams . . . To set out for anywhere, toward Utopia, toward Caphar, Salama, the Islands of the Sun . . . to create all imaginable things from the power of thought; Luczak, that which can be conceived can be created—there are no eternal laws. And get rid of everything unimaginable: get rid of God first of all—because absolute greatness is not imaginable with all the minds in the world. Set time against eternity, science against theology. And then away, away, away with—everything which follows from the idea of the absolute: the power of one man over another, the state, money

. . . adjust relationships in this world to fit the relationship of man to the world. The brain's energy would determine the tempo of a continuous, eternal adjustment . . . Andrzej . . . I had the truth in my hands back then, and I believed . . .

L.: Jerzy . . .

P.: What?

L.: Jerzy's my name, master, Jerzy, not Andrzej!

P.: Who do you think you are? Andrzej or Jerzy: in any case a cipher—a lackey on a run-down estate, a superannuated stable boy, who won't leave a mark behind in this world—you interrupt me for a bagatelle—stand up and straighten up. I command you to listen to me. I'm telling you my life and you're making an issue of your name.

L.: Yes, master, I'm making an issue of my name, Jerzy Luczak —it's the only thing I have—everything else belongs to your excellency.

P.: All right then, let's turn things around—tell me the story of your life!

L.: I hardly have a life.

P.: You're over sixty—you've lived for sixty years . . .

L.: Sixty-four, master, sixty-four.

P.: Sixty-four years of life, tell me about it.

L.: I was born the son of Marek Luczak and Anna Hlaskowa, both serfs in Uladowka. I served your father before you. I had a good head for horses, I don't know where it came from, horses loved me, and I loved them. So I became a stable boy. I remained one for thirty years. When the stable master died I was his successor. That was twenty-four years ago.

P.: Are you married, do you have children?

L.: My wife died in childbirth, the baby died a few days later. (*Softly*) Once I loved a girl, but another man, a freeman farmer, took her away from me.

P.: You said that you were also in Warsaw?

L.: Just once, as your father's coachman.

P.: How long?

L.: Three days . . .

P.: My God, what a life.

L.: My life, master, my life. And I'm satisfied with it. I wouldn't want another. Or perhaps? I've never thought about it. If your grace will continue with the story of his life—it could be that by the end of the story I'd like to change places with him.

P.: A philosopher in servant's clothing! Or a mocker?

L.: Potocki, I don't like it when you ridicule me, not if we are to speak with one another as equals as you demand ... .

P.: My brother, forgive me!

L.: There's nothing to forgive. But I would like . . . to hear the rest of your story. Go on, go on.

P.: The story of my life . . . and if only so that you understand what that is: a master's life, you blockheads. Yes, I was a young gentleman: in a blue frock coat, in yellow trousers, boots of Moroccan leather and shirts of Chinese silk—a count's son from Poland, furnished with a good pension . . . but on my head I wore the red cap of a Jacobin. And I had but one desire, to carry the torch of revolution to Poland, my homeland. To unify and free it. Only in a free country can one think freely, and only free ideas can seize and understand the world . . . but then I saw them cut each other down. The revolution drowned in the blood of the revolutionaries—not freedom but the guillotine had triumphed. Steel was sharper than thoughts—they had cut the head off from the heart on both sides. The heads of the revolution rolled beneath the feet of the mob. It was over—over and done. —So I returned to my country, where else was I to go, if not to my people?

PAUSE

I found them torn apart, powerless, in bondage, without a history or a future.

L.: Each of us has his history—from his father and his grandfather, as far back as we can remember . . .

P.: Yes, each one has his *personal* history. I too have my history —I've read it in the chronicles. The Potocki family is older than the written word, older than Poland, and it drips with blood—but I wanted to know more than my personal history, I wanted to learn *our* history, from the very beginning . . . from the very beginning, when we were not yet divided into master and slave.

L.: That must have been a long time ago, further back than we can remember.

P.: It's come down to us in myths—and lives on in our minds

and hearts. Dreams of the primal mother and lost ballads about white horses, of walking through grass to the end of the world, where the waters plunge into endless space. There was a time when all words were still the words of poetry. That must have been long before language arose from words . . . when words were only whispered, secret words for secret stories of life and death, impressed upon the mind by constant repetition . . . sounds to articulate the passions of the heart and the thrusting movement of thought, as limitless and multilayered as dreams. When man invented signs, letters and forms of writing, and recorded deeds instead of dreams on birch bark and animal skins, scratching on clay tablets or carving in stone, those who had the power of words and speech gained ascendency over the melancholy brooders and dreamers, whose blood became the first ink. The sword was the first chisel, a club the first hammer. The good world of dreams was lost, had been conquered, destroyed, smashed to pieces . . . the world without god, without masters, the world before all revelation, the world of men, was lost. I searched for that lost world . . . with pick and shovel, beneath the earth. For years I traveled about, from the River Oder to the steppes of the Orient, in search of our history. I leveled hills and dug fathom-deep pits—I found castles and fortresses, spear tips, daggers, and arrows, from burial grounds I unearthed bracelets and combs of bronze, silver, gold, and bone, vases of clay and metal, decorated with scenes of murder, war, and violence—mass graves filled with splintered bones and crushed skulls. Sacrificial altars from which the smell of blood still rose after ten thousand years. I sought the primal ground of life and found only death, a thousandfold violent death.

L.: Potocki, you didn't have to search the world to learn that, it is written that man is born to die, that a life of peace exists only in paradise . . .

P.: I was raised by Jesuits, I know those paradises . . . if I had had the strength to be a cynic, I would have made of Uladowka my own personal paradise: I would have been God, and all of you my faithful souls!

L.: Master, you're falling into sin!

P.: If only I were at least still capable of being truly sinful— Jan, Count von Potocki, a Polish Gilles de Rais, a child molester, murderer of small boys and anti-Christ, my scarlet tongue longing for blood, filled to the marrow with the sharp pangs of lust . . . that's the way to make history, that's how you become immortal, by having spread fear and terror, that's how you achieve eternal fame. Who asks a man how humane he is? Kill by the thousands, overthrow empires, burn down the cities of the earth . . . in a thousand years they will still speak of Alexander, of Ivan the Terrible, of Robespierre and Napoleon—you are nothing but ashes, disappearing without a trace, as if you had never lived, suffering for nothing, fifty-four years of suffering for nothing.

L.: You'll have a large tombstone in the Church of the Virgin Mary, with your likeness and your name. You'll lie beside your fathers and your forefathers, and the peasants will cross themselves before your grave, just as they do now before the grave of your father. They will remember you in their prayers . . . while my grave will . . .

P.: Luczak—that is the most terrible fate that I can imagine, and I intend to prevent it. The church is ruthless—what a word: ruth—ruthless with those who have laid hands upon themselves. My place won't be in the transept of the Church of the Holy Virgin, of that you can be sure—no peasant will take off his cap to cross himself before me. I will escape from your prayers, your intercessions, your hollow . . .

L.: May I go now, master? Please let me go. Do you still need the horse?—otherwise I'll unsaddle it and . . .

P.: Stay here, I'm not finished yet—I still have to tell you about my fruitless journies. I'll make it short, and then you can flee back to your miasma of manure and incense. And get a glass there and pour yourself a drink—as long as we're talking man to man, you can't be soberer than I am.

L.: Thanks, I'll have a little glass.

P.: Drink up—you Polacks all have a hollow leg, don't be shy—and prosit!

L.: Prosit!

P.: And another.

———

And prosit!—and another.

L.: And another.

P.: And prosit!—come on now, down the hatch—and another. Now then, now we're even . . . where was I?

L.: Your travels.

P.: My travels . . . I wanted to push to the ends of the civilized world, to see those who lived in eternal snow and those who lived in deserts. I wanted to track down the mystery of the life force . . . but I didn't have the means to arrange for such journies. So I entered the service of Czar Alexander of Russia and traveled on his order throughout that immense empire, taking a census of his peoples. I lived in igloos, in tents, in brushwood huts, and in palaces. In the tents of the nomadic Turkomans—beside the grass fires of the Yakuts, on the steppes of Asia, I found the mystery: the power to live comes from a readiness to accept death.

It's just about to fit . . . a few more seconds . . . now . . .

METALLIC CLICK

. . . at last . . .

BALL ROCKS BACK AND FORTH WITH METALLIC CLICKS

. . . it sounds totally different than I thought it would, it has less bravado . . . metal striking on metal . . .

METALLIC CLICK

nothing like a hymn . . .

METALLIC CLICK

but not banal either . . . on the whole a fine sound.

Hand me the tow and the powder flask! And the ramrod! Can you load a pistol?

L.: No, master.

P.: Haven't you ever been in a duel?

L.: No, master . . .

LOW NOISES: METAL GRATING ON METAL

Dueling is a privilege of the upper classes. We servants fight each other with sticks and stones and kill each other with flails and scythes.

P.: (*Laughing*) You're trying to embarrass me—it won't work, my boy, not any longer. And you won't awaken any new feelings of guilt in me either—fight however and with whomever you wish . . .

L.: The story must be over now . . . I mean, has your grace . . . have you told it to the end?

P.: Where was I . . . With the Turkomans! No, then I haven't finished telling it all, because I lived with them for a long time, and moved about with them over thousands of miles across the grasslands . . . I spent two years in the tent-palaces of Turkoman princes learning the secret language in which they have preserved their myths, stories of another life . . . a life of freedom, equality, and brotherhood. I wrote everything down. But no one at court was interested—my report was hardly acknowledged. Instead they wanted to know the most strategic locations for fortresses, by what routes it would be possible to transport troops without danger, whether the rivers were navigable, where villages and cities could be founded—in short, how the eastern lands could best be explored and settled. They were only concerned with the land, no one wanted to know anything about the people that lived there. Then I turned away. I was very close to death. Everything had been in vain once more. I've written and published a dozen scholarly works, mathematical, geographical, historical, archeological, philological, ethnographical, anthropological . . . there they stand in a neat row, bound in leather and titled in gold: *Voyage en Turquie et en Egypte, Recherches sur la Sarmatie, Voyage dans L'Empire de Maroc, Parades, Fragments historiques et geographiques sur la Scythie, la Sarmatie et le Slaves, Histoire primitive des peuples de Russie, Histoire ancienne de provinces de L'Empire de Russie, Atlas archeologique de la Russie* . . . there they all stand . . . without moving . . . and without having moved anything. Still-births. Fodder for bookworms. Dust . . . from the very beginning. Failures that gave birth to nothing but failure . . . then I put myself in God's place, and created a new world. Here: in over two thousand pages of paper. A paper cosmos—creating men after my own image out of twenty-six letters, forming them with a hundred goosefeather quills and ten liters of ink—the work, not of seven days, but of twelve years—not created out of love—and not out of hate, like the world, but out of fear, out of my fear. Out of fear of life and fear of death . . . for twelve years I lived only by writing. I've grown old in the process. My hair is gray, my teeth have fallen out. My face has become so foreign to me that I can no longer bear to look at myself. I've covered up the mirror—years ago . . . and I've given up trying to defend myself against the falling dust . . . sometimes I open the window of a morning and see suddenly that the trees are blossoming, or have lost their leaves: I hadn't noticed. The external world has become quite foreign to me. But I have conquered myself, the world, and God; with this pile of paper and this silver sphere. It was one and the same work—writing the book—the one great and true book about life—and filing down this ball. Look, Jerzy, my brother, it's perfect, round, gleaming, a noble metal through and through—a work of art, created for myself alone and the equal of my manuscript. So I've placed my hopes on paper and metal, founded my beliefs upon a paradox, Jan Potocki, eternal life upon perishable paper and final obliteration through imperishable metal . . . when everything, everything has fallen to dust, this ball fathoms deep in the earth will remain a trace of my life throughout eternity.

Pour yourself a drink—and one for me . . . prosit!

L.: Prosit!

P.: Throw the glass over your shoulder like a gentleman should.

SOUND OF TWO GLASSES BREAKING

Well then, you were speaking of a servant's happiness. Now go and unsaddle the horse, I won't be needing it anymore today . . . Go on, you may retire—and come back again soon and we'll have another conversation . . . No, don't say anything more. I thank you.

DOOR OPENS AND CLOSES

LONG PAUSE

God of the Christians, old friend, we were interrupted by this man, and now I can't remember what it was I still wanted to say to you. Perhaps it will come to me later.

POURING OF WATER / DRINKING / DRINKING WITHOUT SWALLOWING

THE LOUD SOUND OF A PISTOL SHOT

PUTTING MAKEUP ON EMPTY SPACE

ANNE WALDMAN

I am putting makeup on empty space
all patinas convening on empty space
rouge blushing on empty space
I am putting makeup on empty space
pasting eyelashes on empty space
painting the eyebrows of empty space
piling creams on empty space
painting the phenomenal world
I am hanging ornaments on empty space
gold clips, lacquer combs, plastic hairpins on empty space
I am sticking wire pins into empty space
I pour words over empty space, enthrall the empty space
packing, stuffing, jamming empty space
spinning necklaces around empty space
Fancy this, imagine this: painting the phenomenal world
bangles on wrists
pendants hung on empty space
I am putting my memory into empty space
undressing you
hanging the wrinkled clothes on a nail
hanging the green coat on a nail
dancing in the evening it ended with dancing in the evening
I am still thinking about putting makeup on empty space

I want to scare you: the hanging night, the drifting night,
the moaning night, daughter of troubled sleep I want to
        scare you
I bind as far as cold day goes
I bind the power of 20 husky men
I bind the seductive colorful women, all of them
I bind the massive rock
I bind the hanging night, the drifting night, the
moaning night, daughter of troubled sleep
I am binding my debts, I magnetize the phone bill
bind the root of my sharp pointed tongue
I cup my hands in water, splash water on the empty space
Water drunk by empty space
Look what thoughts will do   Look what words will do
from nothing to the face
from nothing to the root of the tongue
from nothing to speaking of the empty space
I bind the ash tree
I bind the yew
I bind the willow
I bind uranium
I bind the uneconomical unrenewable energy of uranium
dash the uranium to empty space
I bind the color red I seduce the color red to empty space
I put the sunset in empty space
I take the blue of his eyes and make an offering to empty space
renewable blue
I take the green of everything coming to life, it grows &
climbs into empty space
I put the white of the snow at the foot of empty space
I clasp the yellow of the cat's eyes sitting in the
        black space I clasp them to my heart, empty space
I want the brown of one floor to rise up into empty space
Take the floor apart to find the brown,
bind it up again under spell of empty space
I want to take this old wall apart I am rich in my mind
        thinking
of this, I am thinking of putting makeup on empty space

everything crumbles around empty space
the thin dry weed crumbles, the milkweed is blown into
    empty space
I bind the stars reflected in your eye
from nothing to these typing fingers
from nothing to the legs of the elk
from nothing to the neck of the deer
from nothing to porcelain teeth
from nothing to the fine stand of pine in the forest
I kept it going when I put the water on
When I let the water run
sweeping together in the empty space
there is a better way to say empty space
turn yourself inside out and you might disappear
you have a new definition in empty space
what I like about impermanence is the clash
of my big body with empty space
I am putting the floor back together again
I am rebuilding the wall
I am slapping mortar on the bricks
I am fastening the machine together with delicate wire
there is no eternal thread, maybe there is thread of pure gold
I am starting to sing inside about the empty space
there is some new detail every time
I am taping the picture I love so well on the wall
Two parrots seated on the lampshade on a jungle flower
everything illuminated out of empty space
I hang the black linen dress on my body
the hanging night, the drifting night, the moaning night
daughter of troubled sleep
this occurs to me
I hang up a mirror to catch stars, everything occurs to me out
    in the
night in my skull of empty space
I go outside in starry ice
I build up the house again in the memory of empty space
this occurs to me about empty space
that it is never to be mentioned again
Fancy this

imagine this
painting the phenomenal world
there's talk of dressing the body with strange adornments
to remind you of vow to empty space
there's talk of the discourse in your mind like a silkworm
I wish to venture into a not chiseled place
I pour sand on the ground
Objects and vehicles emerge from the fog
the canyon is dangerous tonight
suddenly there are warning lights
The patrol is helpful in the manner of guiding
there is talk of slowing down
there is talk of a feminine deity
I bind her with a briar
I bind with the tooth of a tiger
I bind with my quartz crystal
I magnetize the worlds
I cover myself with jewels
I drink amrita
there is some new detail
there is a spangle on her shoe
there is a stud on her boot
the tires are studded for the difficult climb
I put my hands to my face
I am putting makeup on the empty space
I wanted to scare you with the night that scared me
the drifting night, the moaning night
someone was always intruding to make you forget empty space
you put it all on
you put paint on your nails
you put on your scarves
all the time adorning empty space
        whatever-your-name-is I tell you empty space
with your fictions with dancing come around to it
with your funny way of singing come around to it
with your smiling come to it
with your enormous retinue & accumulation come around to it
with your extras come round to it
with your good fortune, with your lazy fortune come round to it

when you look most like a bird, that is the time to come around
    to it
when you are cheating, come to it
when you are in your anguished head
when you are not sensible
when you are insisting on the
praise from many tongues
It begins with the root of the tongue
it begins with the root of the heart
there is a spinal cord of wind
singing & moaning of empty space

FOUR POEMS

JOAN RETALLACK

THE SECRET LIFE OF GILBERT BOND

first comes the logic of substitution
then the high school class reunion
kinship in Bali
buildings tombs and costumes
complete selection perfecto vignettes

on the British scene
rural clergy in horse green chairs
fondly dubbed the Latin farmer
sky is bland and intrusive
trees are oddly vacant
lawn belabors ones stare

O Hodge the cat
nightgown madness
the ubiquitous pelvic brim
yes the Jewish element in Literature
viral pneumonia marginalia
moice chorsels of puetered noodles
Blaise Pascal sleeves
clarity figs and moral force

EXISTENCE IS AN ATTRIBUTE

A.
1. All I can remember is I thought I heard
2. "jowls of the madonna" on the car radio.
3. We had just passed the sign that says Darnestown.
4. There was a red, white and blue mailbox on the left
5. that said Owens. There was a cardboard box
6. in the middle of the road. It was raining.
7. You said, I can prove you don't exist:
8. If you exist, I can't prove you don't exist.
9. Either you exist or I am proving
10. you don't exist.
11. I am proving you don't exist.
12. You don't exist.

B.
1. All I can remember is I thought I heard
2. "jowls of the madonna" on the car radio
3. as we passed the sign that says Darnestown, 8 mi.
4. I knew it couldn't be right, "jowls."
5. You said you were going to prove I didn't exist.
6. This is no idle threat, you said, laughing;
7. logic forces you to certain conclusions.
8. It was raining hard, mud washing onto the road.
9. All I can remember is "jowls," though I knew
10. only a split second later it couldn't be right.
11. You swerved to avoid what turned out to be
12. a box in the middle of the road.

Read A&B combined as follows:

A – 1
B – 1

A – 2
B – 2

A – 3
B – 3

etc.

SEE IT AND SAY IT IN ENGLISH

The night thickens like marzipan.
Your brioche smile.
If you don't know Dada
you're doomed to repeat it.
The chief duty of the lids
is to keep a film of tears
spread over the eye.
This fact is not per se melodramatic.
But the world is a narrow strip
like traveling through fog in a train.
Gimmie one, red shoes walking, BLT, coke.
I go often to the cinema.
It is difficult to find words to describe.
We have so many friends in Paris.
How long have you been here?
How is the weather?

THE ADVENTURE OF DIALECTIC

The mouth.
To survive, animals must eat. In search of food, they advance,
mouth-end foremost. Around the mouth, the organs of special
sense are developed. Hence, the brain establishes itself at the
mouth-end of the body.

"Is there a cure for Kansas?"
Is that a feather in my stir-fry dinner?
Your shadow rests
on the graph of the kitchen tile.
Yes, it is vain
to hope for Eternity
by Aenigmaticall Epithetes.
Better to pour the wine
and go on with dinner.

No, there is no cure for Kansas
if by, "Is there a cure for Kansas?"
you mean: So much more
comes into the mind
than can be let into the house
or the conversation.
I attempt with slivers of ginger
to awaken your tongue
as the sun at noon
illustrates all shadows.

But the sky is a pullman
pulling Wichita into the station
at 5:30 A.M.
This is the starting point.
The hunter is there in his waders
and the Dr. of forensic medicine.
We gulp down coffee and smoke
focusing the runaway circles
of our mouths and eyes.

THE PALACE OF KANDAHAR

RUSSELL HALEY

When you turn westwards from the largest city in this country you encounter a long low range of hills. The hills arose by volcanic action seventeen million years ago and are now severely eroded, covered in bush. The highest point is no more than five hundred meters above sea level.

By day you see a scattering of new houses among the dark green of vegetation. But at night you observe the private lights of these dwellings. A dome of yellow light is always suspended over the densely occupied central area of the city and so the points of illumination in the ranges seem brighter than the stars.

Things . . . erode, change, become clothed. A volcanic island sprang up in the harbor seven hundred years ago and now Rangitoto is covered in green.

By day, in the city, the eye longs for the hills not to be there. If that were so the eye could run out, unchecked, and find its rest in the unbounded sea.

The range is not merely a barrier to sight. The early settlers hated the hills. Scarcely anyone now expresses fear or hatred of the range but it marks a point of change, of transition. Beyond the houses on the eastern flanks of the hills there is second-growth bush—manuka, flax, tree ferns, nikau palms, rangiora, and toi-toi grasses—and there are pockets of native forest, tall rimu trees, and even larger kauri. There are no human habitations here—you do not find those until you reach the coastal strip.

47

The bush runs right to the coast, to the dizzying heights of the headlands where the earth itself has dropped away to be changed and transformed by the restless energy of the tides. Grit has fined down to sand and rock to the wave-turned sculpture of pebbles.

Great drifts of black sand have been built by the wind.

Roads and tracks run through the bush beyond the barrier of the range. Some of the tracks have been here for more than a hundred years and many of them run to creeks which coil through the valleys in the hills.

A hundred years ago this area was intensively milled, the larger creeks were dammed, and the massive trunks of kauri were floated to the sea. Certain dams remain in part, the creek waters running clear through their timbers, as evidence of the logging. These timbers have not rotted. In the sun which slants in through the bush the man-shaped structures are a silver-gray. They will be there in another hundred years.

After the timber-workers moved away farmers came and tried to clear and burn the land for crops of potatoes or to run sheep. The bush has returned, the farms have gone, the tracks remain.

These tracks through the bush have the same complexity as animal trails. They turn and wind and shift and rise and fall. They are a process. They seem to lead nowhere.

You come to a rise where the heat shimmers from the glaze of green bush and though you know the sea is *there,* out, out, the eye catches at the white underside of a leaf and becomes locked and tangled in a denser and more complex world than the turning and lifting waves.

People from the city become lost in their walks. They are pursued by the notion of destination and believe in geometry. There are no dangerous animals in the bush.

It is said that the people who live on this side of the range keep no mirrors in their houses. They are solitary and reclusive and all seem old. No one is married.

What is true is that there are dwellings to be found, some formally owned, others taken by right of squatting, along the intricate network of smaller human tracks.

Unlike the geometrical expressions of desire depicted in the scattered houses of the range, homes whose façades are deliberately turned to the world, the city, these places in the coastal bush articulate another need. They appear to be tuned to solitude but in essence they make a statement about the self.

The statement is misread by the people from the city. The sheds and baches are ramshackle, even disgusting, and the people who live in them are nothing but aged hermits. The houses do not say: I am solitary, alone. They say: I have rejected you. I have found something else.

Harley's bach, unlike mine, is within the sound of the sea. He owns his cottage. Mine is a temporary refuge. When he first came to this coast and bought his land he found a pocket of scoria and so his house has foundation walls of stone, weatherboard cladding to the eaves, and a roof of tin.

He carried the boards through the bush and he dragged the roofing iron along the tracks. His house is one large room. In one corner he has a bed of webbing and poles. At the farthest distance away from the bed he cooks on a cast-iron stove. The stove was moved down through the paths in sections and then bolted together by Harley.

When the stove leaks smoke into his room Harley pastes the cracks with clay.

I know this because I have been with Harley when he has done it.

I'll bring you a small bag of cement, I told Harley.

He pasted the cracks with clay and made no reply. Certainly there is no mirror in Harley's house.

Beside Harley's bed on a wooden box there is a telephone. The bach has no electricity. The instrument is black and of a long outmoded design. It is an unofficial telephone. Harley pays no bills. I have never heard it ring in Harley's house. Not until today, that is.

Today was one of those times when I thought I might bypass Harley on my walk through the bush. My intention was to reach the northern headland, turning inland by the black lake in the volcanic cone, and then to spend the day in search of the Palace of Kandahar.

Rumors abound about this place. Garnet has said she remembers an inlaid floor. As a child of seven, she says, they swept the marble floor with ponga fronds and danced. She talks of the feel of her grandmother's arms, her black lace dress.

Garnet is Harley's oldest friend. She lives a two-hour tramp away from here in her bach on Pole Line Ridge.

What seems certain is that an Afghani came here to live in 1880. He'd made a fortune from gold and camels on his great Australian treks. The marble was brought by bullock cart from Northland—the inlays made by a craftsman trained in Agra. Our history goes deeper than we care to admit. There is blood in the land. Walk for an hour and you come to the place where the local Maori tribe was slaughtered. Grendel might live in the black volcanic lake of Wainamu.

But my footsteps turned. I paused. Harley was raising his arm and his hammer. An animal hung from a wire in his yard. I was stilled by that hieratic gesture. He struck and the animal swung and bled. I . . . live without flesh. Harley has different needs from mine.

Tucker, he said. His evening meal. The opossum spun on its wire; the blood from its head made a circle in the earth. I have seen them feigning death on the roads that lead to here. Their eyes gleam red in the lights of cars while stray cat's eyes shine green.

Go on in, he smiled, I'll skin it while you rest.

The skin flays back in a way you would not think. We emerge naked and raw into light.

Sometimes in my quiet evenings I think of that Afghani camel driver's death. Did he, I wonder, kneel and turn his back on sea and falling sun? On his floor. The inlays cold and faintly ridged under his hands. Or did he drift into sleep and irritating dreams of insects, flesh?

Harley, in deference to my taste, had draped a sugar bag around the slaughtered animal. The telephone rang. With every phrase he uttered Harley looked straight at me. I have never seen eyes like his. They are the clearest, faintest blue. I think they are so clear and straight because they have not looked at a mirror in forty years.

Garnet, he said. She thinks she might have done her hip.

In the first stretch we had to climb. Harley in the lead. Birds hovered close to him as though he were not a man, walking. I wish he had told me their names. Instead, he talked of Garnet.

Her old man used to tie her on the horse, he said, not turning. After a day in town she'd be bent, arse on sideways in the pub. He'd follow, humping a flagon and his gun. Every man he met he offered him a drink. By the time they got back here she was raging dry with thirst and he'd done the flagon in. Imagine meeting an old coot with a rifle and a gallon jar. You'd jump to take your turn.

Garnet lay on the floor by her illegal telephone—patched in by a friendly lineman on the Ranger's wire because he often came out here to fish and knew these two were friends.

Let's have you up then for a start and into bed.
You're not to see me, Garnet said. You're not to see me under there.
Wouldn't do me any good if I did, said Harley and lifted her like a small bag of wheat.
Oh Christ! I felt it click.
Just as I thought, Harley said. Your knee and not your hip. That's twice you've had me out for your knee. A bit of cartilage knocking on the bone.
I used to dance, Garnet said pulling up her eiderdown, I used to dance as good as anyone.
At the Palace? I wondered.
Everywhere, Garnet said.

We walked back with Garnet's home-made wine singing in our heads.

She did as well, Harley said. As light as a fantail.

Harley pushed cut sections of manuka into his stove. There is a grace in the familiar routine. Each stick was cleanly chopped.

Getting dark, Harley said. You can camp over there by the stove if you like.

Listen to an old man sleeping and you cannot help but know where you are going. And the sea and the wind tell you the same. My place is behind a hill. I do not feel the shake of the largest waves nor the steady push of the southwest wind.

But Harley's, built in rock, shuddered and moaned—his house a larger image of his turbulent and clashing sleep. How can he turn and turn when he is so steady by day?

You won't you know, he said in his sleep. You won't.

. . . and I moved slowly up one of the headland tracks. Dense bush on my right and nothing but a broken fence on my left. I heard her voice crying out from below the level of the road. It wasn't fear. It was a sound I hadn't heard in years.

The side fell down in a vertical field. A field prepared by man for his use but canted, tipped hopelessly down to the sea below. And in the only purchase in a corner of the field she stood with her back against the broken fence.

The man is thrusting at her as they both stand precariously above the void. He is obscured by the folds of her coat which she holds out with her arms on either side of him and curving inwards around his back. She opens her mouth for another cry and I see the great set wings of her hair.

Our field of vision to the left is entirely blank.

She feels his climax, not as he might imagine it as a hot, needle-sharp pang striking against a wall of soft tissue, but as a loosening, a warmth, a relaxing.

I am both in and not in the vision. Present and not present. A manipulator who cannot act. An obscure consciousness which tries to direct but which is rigidly determined.

The image fades and is brought back. She has a large white face, emphasized by the permanently waved hair which is dark, parted on one side, and which sweeps out from the sides of her head in those tightly massed wings. Her lipstick is almost black in this light. All of us know that at the moment of climax their legs would have been weak and trembling, the void somehow closer.

He hopes that as he withdraws something of her nakedness will be revealed, that there might be some gleam of white light in the darkness, but the coat is folded rapidly around her body. No matter how my attitude on the track alters that cloaking occurs.

They fall upwards out of the edge of sight. Day breaks in like a pool where I lie on the floor of Harley's bach.

Another night, Harley says. In this coagulated light of morning I have to agree with him, his tone.

As I prepare to leave Harley tells me that as he goes out to fish by the three rocks he often sees people from the city naked on the beach.
They roll around in the surf like white seals, he tells me.

As you leave Harley's bach you have to cross his creek by a fallen tree. It is lodged against rocks on either side. In summer when the stream is low the water flows under the log. In winter the creek rises over the trunk and his bridge is impassable.
Winter and summer though you can use the ford on the far side of Harley's island. This way takes you through the nikau grove and you arrive at the beach at its northernmost extremity.
If he were to visit me, in winter, he would have to make a southward journey, passing through three bays and from the final one where the mussel beds are best, he would find the path leading to the saddleback and eventually my corrugated-iron shack at the rear of the hill, located in a clearing among the ti-trees.
He came once. I offered him rice and dhal, the only food I had in the place. Harley looked through me with his pale eyes.
There's a bag of mussels outside, he said.

I broke my rule and ate with him. We cooked them in their own water on a bare iron plate over a small fire of manuka. I have never enjoyed a meal more. When the shellfish opened in the heat they did not seem like flesh although they were the color of a fading bruise. They did not seem like meat.

Now I make repeated journeys to the closest, the best of the bays. I gather mussels.

I crossed the log but instead of cutting up through the bush I headed along the creek path which leads to the beach.

Birds elude me in their names. I know the tui and the tern—but what were those small dancing birds with yellow heads who accompanied me on my walk? Harley would know.

I must make a stronger effort to discover the names of living things.

Light dances on the creek water. The wind makes small waves. I hear a throaty cry from the beach in the distance and stop. The vertical field drops away on my left. I am saved from falling by the name of a living thing. A swallow bursts from my left corner of vision and swoops over the stream. They are nesting in the caves which might have been used by the Maori settlers for storing food.

The creek widens; the plumes of toi-toi are at their finest color, and I approach the point where, at high tide, fresh and salt water mingle.

I edged across the final stretch of rocks to the drifted bank of black sand.

A naked girl-child no more than a year old and browner than my hand tottered towards the edge of the lagoon and fell face down. I picked her up and she struggled like an eel. Her mother advanced on me, as naked as the child, and took her from my arms. The skin of her forearm touched mine.

Thanks, she said. Her hair was blond, curled, and lay very close to her skull.

I wanted to say, it is my pleasure, but the internal words sounded oddly obscene. I smiled instead and hoped that my eyes did not appear to be looking through her like Harley's.

The tide was high. I had to struggle to reach my final bay. There is a part where you have to edge across a short face of rock and the waves slap at your feet. The first two bays are of the black volcanic sand so dense with iron you can lift it with a magnet but this southernmost one is a pebble beach. It was utterly deserted.

I built a cairn of pebbles as high as it was possible to go. Then I stepped back twenty paces at least, stooped for smaller pebbles— odd the intensity of choosing stones which will weigh comfortably and fit the hand—and then I began to throw pebbles at my cairn. I do not choose to count the number of times I missed. A man on a deserted beach throwing rocks at something he has built.

The dream, the cairn, Garnet's displaced knee, and Harley's muttered dream-speech all gathered in my mind so that, as I approached my own bach, it seemed foreign to me. My hand went to the wrong side of the door when I reached for the string latch.

I cannot seem to overcome this sense of displacement. I feel almost as that Afghani must have felt when he first heard the musical but oddly throttled cry of the tui. He must have imagined that it was an irreverent and mechanical toy placed there in the bush for his discomfort.

The patterns of the inlaid floor in the fabled Palace of Kandahar are said to resemble nothing alive created by God on this earth.

Perhaps tomorrow I will set out again on this day's distracted quest.

I have heard that in the Australian bush there are circles of beaten earth, so firm and hard they might resemble marble, where the cassowary birds perform their mating dances.

I am racked again. This time I am hiding, part submerged, in tepid water. Two women whom I have never seen before accuse me of unknown crimes. Before I fell asleep an opossum was uttering its hoarse and breathless cries to the night. I walked from my bed to the window. The bush crowds so close I cannot see the range of hills which separates this coast from the city. But in the sky, to the east, I could see an immense yellow dome of light.

In spite of the barrier range, day by day the city seems closer. More people are coming to our beach whatever the difficulties of moving down the paths. I hear them grumbling on their return, on their climb—Why can't the authorities lay down roads to the beach?

I reverse my journey of yesterday. Across the saddleback and down the hill. I look out over the sea, westwards towards invisible Australia, and notice for the very first time that on the high rocky island with the hole pierced in its center, an island that looks like a castle seen in a dream, there is a tree growing.

We live in this world which is familiar only to the extent that it is not apprehended. The tree has obviously been there for years. Now it is a different island. Where is the island that I have been looking at all this time? I understand at last why we who have chosen to be here have destroyed our mirrors. Could we continue to live with the person that we might see?

There are more naked people on the beach. Yesterday, half the crowd was unclothed. Today, the mob is bigger. It is Anniversary Day and at least three-quarters of them are nude.

Two girls pass me on their way to the water. Their faces are impassive. They have great strength in hip and thigh.

I too walk down to the tide's edge. A wave has passed leaving a bright glaze. I look down. The sun is behind my back. I hunch in silhouette. Not a single feature can be discerned.

Harley's door is closed. There is no smoke from his chimney. The opossum skin is pegged out on a board to dry. I can look at it. Harley must have gone to visit Garnet.

I see her dancing on the Palace floor. The marble is circled by a mound of swept leaves. She is seven years old. Her mouth opens to speak to her grandmother but an inarticulate cry escapes. She is naked and browner than my arm.

I climb up the narrow bush track taking care to walk as silently as possible. A fantail almost brushes my face. In the scrub at the side of the path I can hear, at intervals, the small cries of young quails. They are as foreign here as the swallows I saw yesterday but they are here to stay. I know their names.

Near the top of the path where it dips and is crossed by a small creek I smelled the unmistakable odor of human shit. I have already counted two plastic bags and a cigarette box. Now there is shit by water.

I cast around until I find where it is. There has been no attempt to cover what has been left. It lies at the edge of the water. There is no need to trace the small creek down in my mind. I know already that it feeds into Harley's stream.

I remove it. I . . . erase it.

I prepare food. I have washed several times. I prepare my food and smell my hands. Harley is of great concern to me. No, not because of the feces. The running creek will have purified any filth. But the journey to Garnet's bach is long for someone of his age. He could telephone but I know that he would not. Tomorrow I will call again.

The tree on the island is still there. I edge along the footholds in the rock face which takes me to the next bay. I reach out, without looking, with my left hand. The knob of rock which I always hold is not there. Instead there is a yellow scar in the face of the rock. I look closely at the fresh mark. Above the scar where the knob has broken away there is a white mark of impact. Someone has deliberately smashed away the handhold. It takes a little more effort to move on—a more tentative reaching out.

The crowd has dropped away since it is no longer a holiday in the city. Yet there are still a large number of people on the beach.

I can count on one hand the number of couples who are clothed.

But now they are not simply naked. I see pairs, not always men and women, lying amongst the dunes. They are pressed closely together, touching each other intimately. They are not copulating but they touch each other with slow and dreamy gestures. There are no children.

Harley's door is still closed. He does not lock his bach. Still, I feel hesitant about going into his house. It might seem like an invasion. He could be ill though, incapable of movement or speech.

There was no sign of Harley. His stove was cold. I operated the device which allowed me to bypass the city exchange and telephoned Garnet.

He's not here. Haven't seen him since you were both out. My knee's better.

But where is Harley? Surely not in the city. His needs, like all of ours, are provided by the sea, his fine garden netted against the opossums, and the traveling shop which calls once a fortnight and stays for two hours back up over that ridge on the main road eastwards.

I prowled his garden like a trespasser. His tomatoes required water. I knew then that he had not planned a long stay away from his home. His vine arbor was hanging with clusters of grapes just beginning to turn in color.

Harley has a corrugated-iron tank fed by a sheet-metal catchment in the bush. I uncoiled the hose and watered his garden. The pressure was surprisingly good. The plants immediately wilted but they will recover. Better to water in the sun than not at all.

I tried the path to the deep-drop toilet. The door creaked open on a cool silence. No one was there.

Harley is much neater than I. There is nothing out of place. The canvas bag in which he collects his mussels is hanging, dry, behind the door.

I return home by the bush track. There is fresh excrement by the small creek. I would weep for us all if it were possible. Instead, I clench myself and move what must be moved.

I made the same journey and search for the following three days. Still no Harley. I telephoned Garnet again. She too is concerned but less so than I.

You haven't known him as long as I have, Fergie. He takes off but he never says where, Garnet cackled. He goes because he never gets any change out of me. He'll be back. Don't worry your head.

They drift in silently through the night and surround my house. The walls are transparent and I am illuminated from within. Everything I do can be seen. I wash my hands but they will not go away. I decide I will ignore them. They make no noise but I know that they are there.

Massive clouds streaming over from the southwest this morning. Like being plunged deeply into ocean water and watching the progress of a herd of whales overhead. There is scarcely any sun. The pebbles on the beach are dull. I cast around for one to throw but nothing seems to fit my hand.

The tree has burst into bloom on the island. I can see the blood-red flowers. It must be a pohutukawa tree seeded on some massive tide. Or by a bird. But the tree is two months out of season—it should have flowered in November and not in late January. The message of the tree is insistent. Most pohutukawas are dying on our coast. They are killed by the opossums who eat their leaves. Not so this one. At the lowest tide there is no causeway to that island. It is moated and secure. But the tree gleams red and it is a foreign color against the iron-gray sea and the dark rock.

It survives and is solitary.

I can hear voices before I round the difficult corner. They are convulsive cries akin to crows and seagulls but less human than those birds.

Ah aiee ah ah eeh eh ah oh oh aiee aiee oh!

The city crowd is swarming on the beach. They are single, twos and threes, and larger groups. As I step down from the rocks a solitary man is masturbating against the stones. He has a vivid tattoo on his right arm and the image moves as he moves. The tattoo depicts a naked woman copulating with a snake.

I must move carefully. Excrement is dotted on the beach. A couple roll in locked embrace as I pass. The beach is filled with plunging bodies and with garbage. Cans and discarded clothing are heaped in piles. Their bodies are smeared thickly with iron sand.

I might easily have been wrong. It must suffice to say that intuitions come at us unawares. Yet at the edge of vision, stooped, running, head cast over one shoulder, pale eyes blank yet feral, I believed I saw the naked image of a man I thought I knew.

The door of the house on the island was open. I did not call.

Almost impossible to utter now. I approached the small creek, trembling. The stream had been dammed with stones and twigs, sods and a plastic sheet. In the expanding pool behind the dam human excrement floated.

My wants are simple. Again, I will abstain from flesh. One day I will see Harley again as he used to be. I will talk to him. There would be an end to these dreams. And a silent, empty beach.

Each evening the dome of yellow light grows larger and more intense over the city to the east. It is transmitting dreams like some gigantic machine. But surely the Palace would be cold and remote—solitary and silent. I called on Garnet, alone, and obtained a clearer image of the site of the Palace.

It'll be nothing, she said. At the best a clear patch of grass.

I looked at her and made no reply. My gaze was as firm as Harley's used to be, before the flesh entered him, and it was as opaque of meaning.

What a sleep I had the night before! Desert country which I shared with a myriad of insects: shield bugs, locust, the giant and grotesque weta . . . and an airplane fragmented into a million parts. A long scar rippled down my side. I must repair the vehicle and fly from this place. But the raw and shattered edges would not match.

I rose once at three in the morning. The light was so brilliant I had to keep my eyes closed. I could see through the very membranes of my eyelids.

I sank back to my hopeless activity of reconstruction.

There is one bend in the path on the way to the Palace of Kandahar where you can see clear down to the creek and Harley's bach. A thin blue column of ti-tree smoke issued from his chimney.

I struck on through the bush, through the empty tracks, for the Palace.

Turns that deny the linear insistence of the mind. The path to which I fought my way might not even have been of human origin. These hills have been here for seventeen million years. I was reckless of finding my way out again.

At one point a late-flowering kowhai confused me with the color of a golden dome.

I penetrated further into that hinterland than I ever had before.

Green! You cannot use that word so infinite is the variety in the bush. I was enveloped in every shade and bathed in the noise of insect life. The sound rose and fell in my ears. Behind the liquid bubble of the tui and the fantail's agitated twitter, in a great reverberating sweep, was the massed song of the male cicada.

I paused to watch one crackle on a tree. He was surrounded by the body cases of his former selves. I touched his wings and he clicked and sprang away.

Harley has told me something of their forms. The larvae burrow in the earth where they feed off the roots of trees. They are whiter than naked, etiolated flesh. But they armor themselves in the earth and emerge. Another transformation and they leave their horny cases glued to trees. They come out of themselves to sing.

I found a clearing ringed by huge pohutukawa trees. So far from the coast and so profuse they must have been set by human hand.

They had not been damaged by the opossums. Below the trees thick drifts of scarlet filaments covered the ground.

I believe I had discovered the Palace of Kandahar. There was no marble, no fluted columns or golden dome. Simply a level clearing in the bush surrounded by the giant trees.

And a peace which goes beyond the power of human words.

I dozed, dreamless in the shade.

Near subaural, catching at the very edge of human sound, I heard them coming. The Palace should have been my last redoubt but how can you defend your eyes, your ears, your skin.

Faintly at first, but swelling, drowning out the insect song, my voice, the naked city people came, filling the air with their tumultuous roar.

Aiee ah ah oh aiee oh ah!

I should have been a pale white thing—to slip down sideways in the earth. But Harley led the dance. There was great confusion —milling crowds. I felt an inarticulate cry escape my throat.

I might have escaped. Escaped! But for the sight of those set wings of hair, the large white face.

I *fought* to take my place in line.

Aiee aiee oh oh ah eh ah oh oh aiee aiee ah!

I grow erect. I plunge.

These hills have been here for seventeen million years. Things erode quickly here. The skin flays from my spine.

We advance back on the city in our naked lines. We will invest it for a thousand years. We are not solitary. We are not alone.

We reject nothing.

TWO POEMS

EDWIN BROCK

PORTRAIT OF A LADY

Always on midsummer day she sits behind
drawn curtains complaining of the sun;
outside her fuschias die of drought
and the attention of a small slug

in the afternoon her children come
one by one for their birthright kiss
which she dispenses like a pale fuschia
dying of drought and respectability

from the folds of her curtains she hears
the neighbours noisily making love and
rehearses the complaint she will bring to
the blind councilor who receives complaints

on the nineteenth of December she sends
Christmas cards and other cards on appropriate
dates; then waits for the arrival of her
own cards which are late and torn by slugs

she checks her tin clock by the radio
at the radio's hourly time-checks

and shakes it in case the slugs have laid
little mountains of round white eggs

when the love-making neighbours noisily
climax her TV protests with frenetic lines
which she reports to the councilor whose eyes
blink from a glass at the side of her bed.

OUR WAR

We stopped on Hong Kong's
winding coastal road and the
Chinese driver showed us foxholes

I remember scraps of uniform but not
whether the bones and dogmeat flesh
were fact or fiction

it is Christmas in Hong Kong
in 1946 at the end of
the war we just missed

I do not remember celebration
unless the NAAFI sold mince pies
or we gave each other cards

or plunged ourselves into
the sacking-draped beds
where pox was sold and

the old married men carried
it back to the sickbay
in paper, singing carols.

SEVEN POEMS

MICHAEL RECK

LES SALUTS

I
Mr. Glicknips, hello!
we're on the radio.

Hello, Annie, hello, Jim
with the saints and cherubim,

you, old Jubjub, you, J. Paws,
keep the *nomos,* keep the laws,

and the funny guy in the gray suit
gets a salute,

for the cat in the broad cravat
a tip of the hat,

hello to the distinguished gent
who sells 24 kinds of liniment,

Marcelino with the broad behind
and Mildred delicate as wind

and you, Dr. Norman Peale,
I shall someday reveal

the spiritual manna
of your dark arcana,

and Billy and Amy, Johnny and Joe,
hello, hello, hello, hello.

II
Goodbye to that sinister chap over there
skulking behind his chair

to Bubbles, whose breasts flop,
as she serves dinner, in our soup

goodbye to Mr. Pickwick Squirms
and a million other little worms

and all straight-laced society
who watch for our sobriety

to Eva with housebroken ducks
and piles and piles of unread books

to that foul scientist who sent
a spaceship in the firmament

and Skonky Bones and Charlie Chuff
who'll learn someday if they wait enough

to tightrope artist Arthur B.
who took his tumble manfully

and that awful fellow Freud
goodbye, goodbye, I'll take a ride

into the sempiternal sky,
goodbye, goodbye, goodbye, goodbye.

ACADEMIA

I learned a lot from my
Professor Boring—he was,
but never mind, no one's
to blame for his name. There I

sat in the last row of
Sanders Theater as Boring
droned on. I learned rats with long
tails were less likely to

I've forgotten—anyhow,
I learned all there is to know
about rats. I learned they're so
yes of course no

one's responsible for
his name but due to that
course in dear old Harvard more
than thirty years ago

I can't endure psychology.
Rats do not interest me.
I find the whole damn thing
infinitely—you know.

A LOOK BACK

O I remember those lovely days
Washington A.D. forty-four
our heroic soldiers waging war
to save the world for Uncle Joe
and the Gulag Archipelago

Jesus Christ was Dwight D. Ike
Emily Post the Holy Ghost

it was such fun when a German town
went up like nothing in the air
O those were the days when we loved war

FDR's least burp at a fireside chat
put my dad in ecstasy, he thought
the heavens had opened when Eleanor
showed her incisors to the poor
O those were the days when we loved war

with Harriman rushing off to see
how men might be forever free
for capital and the Cominform
we prayed for arms the Lord gave more
O those were the days when we loved war

next to God there was deMOCKracy
and of course the armaments industry
we said "when Socialism comes
the dear dear people will have the plums"
and we all wept little atom bombs

WHORING WITH THE MUSES

Who's this
emerging from the lovehouse
about midnight
muffled in his overcoat—
some celebrity of stage & screen?
some notable of the political scene?

How may we explain
the uneasy cough, the shifty eyes
over the upturned collar,
the evasiveness
of gesture, motion, word?
Why does he avoid the light?

It is your Poet
to whom the Muses
have murmured.
He is bound to the strictest discretion
for the matter admits of no easy
expression.

Slants, winks, and becks
are necessary
to his style.
Only so may he reveal
what the Muses tell
their lover.

Each trade has its tricks
which excuses
midnight visits to the Muses.
He has, after all, paid
and his trade
is another.

SINCE I WEIGH TWO-EIGHTY

wear size twelve shoes
stomach one vast wobble
biceps leached by booze

since my protozoic mind
grows
in a kind of ooze

and my flaccidity
staggers human
credibility

with nothing
gross
as my fun

I want verse slender
hacked in harder
stone.

IDIOCY

Being the only American not to own TV
at times the loneliness creeps
into the corner
where every other American's
beeps.

I don't know a single star,
for celebrities I'm zero,
in all mass communication
it's hard to imagine anything
I know.

I'm so
ignorant it appalls
the citizenry
crouched before their flickery
glow,

they pity me and find
it means a dull mind
to be
televisionarily
blind

and many a coin slips
into the cup
I keep,
it's such a shock to meet
an idiot.

Like Oedipus I wander
happy if when my eyes
rise
to the skies
they are as blank as these.

VIXEN

The lady with fox eyes
regarded me
as if I were some especially
succulent marmot.

Her fox paws
stretched tentatively toward
mine, her fox
claws excited me as

she scratched.
I like this lady, she
cannot read but catches
prey with consummate

finesse. I like her soft
fox lope, fox hair,
fox gaze when the
pupils narrow

fox teeth and fox
legs when she curls
at night in her fox
lair, her fox way of

seeing, keen fox
ears but most of all I
believe I like the way she
fox.

SIX POEMS

ROBIN GAJDUSEK

Dis-
    traught. This is what ought
                to be said. What the thought
re-
  nounces, what
        the pen claims from the
                page, the white
page, what
      the body nets to it-
            self from the passing flood.
I, too,
    as accidental as A-
            pril, in April recovered my-
self in my laugh-
        ter; I was by
           what my pockets dis-
covered, by my as-
        semblage of hands.
                What a boy was in
A-
  pril, what a boy may
        be I could not be
           other. Now

words are my
                deeds, I have no dis-
                                guises, my ways
are my shape,
            I am gathered to-
                            gether, I make myself whole
in my dis-
            traught laughter.

Down range of me is Eden—
                            my sights
                                        fouled, my gun-
finger
        frozen. Who is to blast that cas-
                                    tellated abbey
from its em-
                inence, its mas-
                            tery, spin Adam
                                        and e-
very other dis-
                astrously em-
                            barked pil-
                                    grim
                                        some leagues be-
yond Nod to an-
                other em-
                        bassy?
                            Who is to see
                                        some
pre-
    figured kingdom, some
                        pos-
                            sible heaven?
                                        What home
can be given, dis-
                covered be-
                        yond us?

Their laughter
                    was shaping the room—
                                   I did not know how to leave or
enter,
          not knowing where the real walls were,
                                        until I heard that author-
itative scaffold being built, the frame
                                   of window and door, un-
til I found the center
                    and a place to become
                                   silent. There, in that one
balanced core
          of the structuring nightmare,
                                        I became secure, sham-
ing the echoing fear,
                    the chorus of un-
                                        burdening seeming;
there—dreaming—in that far
                              circle at center,
                                   I fell beyond their sum-
ming song, leaving
                    the world outside and coming
                                   home to myself, in my own
bound tomb, coming
                    home and to loving
        .   wherever I am.

How still the silence lies a-
                              bout the lips and eyes
of a killed grace, de-
                    stroyed face, a spelled a-
                                        sleep child.
Here, not unlike the ways
                    the wind turns a-
                                   bout the fallow field,

leav-
    ing in a dis-
        grace of loneliness the
            loveless flowers,
the hands of this man a-
        bandon re-
          sonance, the re-
assurance
    of touch, make much
        of themselves, ac-
           knowledge
at least the
    ambiance
      of the o-
        ther far but bro-
          ken half.
Be-
  tween
    the broken waves
      of the en-
        rounding air,
the ab-
    stract dream cries "Brother!" and
        "brother!" The lovers
can see, can ap-
    peal to their sea-
      son only as lone-
liness
    reports their rude
      rup-
        ture.

Did you think that one
      could confront the darkness
and not release
    a power of the darkness,
      did you for a moment believe

that internal action
                    did not call forth ghosts, presences
                                        in the flesh, sud-
denly there, become ac-
                    tual, ready to the pre-
                                        pared hand, the un-
veiled eyes?
                    How could you sign on to a voyage
                                        without a premonition
of danger, of the pos-
                    sibilities—a mad captain,
                                        an ice-bound boat, be-
calmed in strange and pes-
                    tilential waters? What du-
                                        ty is there to toil at the oars
to the point of ap-
                    parent found-
                                        ering, of ex-
                                                            haustion—then to a-
bandon the rud-
                    derless craft for re-
                                        turn to safe and gentle wa-
ters? O Mariners!

He had not meant
                    to die; it was all
an error, the sky
                    was descending like love
not wrath,
                    though he had no terror
of death
                    but death's aftermath, what would fall
upon him.
                    It lacked precedent
                                        or proof

and he had no provision for it,
                              not a-
dequate love
              or even faint faith.
                              He would meet
his God like a homing
                  stranger,
                              pro-
digal,
      speechless
                  and uninvited.
                              Assuming
he lived beyond
              the border,
                              what Lord had he
but his ranging
              spirit, his life-
                              filled blood
in his ordered hands,
                  his habit of breath
that he understood.

A DIET OF WORMS

URSULE MOLINARO

Amanda is sitting at her dresser, applying eye shadow, when the peephole forms in her mirror. A small, lidded mound, at eye level, not unlike the peephole in her apartment door, when it is closed. Before a slight pressure of thumb & index finger causes the dull metal lids to part, affording a limited outlook on a glossy green stairway, with a cluster of obese garbage bags slumped in the right-hand corner of her landing.

—Brusquely obscured by the ominous bulk of a delivery man, whom she sees magnified into a mugger before she lets him in.

The peephole in her mirror blinks open automatically; at the pressure of her stare. Disclosing a tunneled view onto a pumice-gray spiral staircase, wrought of dust. 444 pumice-gray dust steps, spiraling from 1980 to 1536,* which give slighty as she climbs them with her eyes. & enters an early-16th-century study, doorless & open to the front like the rooms of dollhouses. With a wall-to-wall carpet of moss.

Where he sits. On a carved oak chair, at a slanted carved oak lectern, piled high with the books he has written. A pewter pitcher of Burgundy at his right elbow. His feet in a muffler of leaves.

He shivers from the draft caused by the hole in her mirror, & touches his beaver-brimmed cap with spider fingers, to make it sit more warmly on his thinker's hair.

* Year of Erasmus' death (in Basel, July 12, 1536)

78

Which Amanda knows   intimately   although her own hair
is thick; dyed a copper glow. Her hand goes up to it, for reassur-
ance; mirroring his gesture as she shivers with him.

A shiver of recognition. Because she knows the seated man,
every line in the pensive pumice-gray face.

—She shares his expensive tastes in clothes & food. His love of
chewy, velvet-smooth Burgundy. With which he tried to appease
his cranky stomach.

Amanda's own stomach tenses with the sudden projection of a
dull nagging pain, a veil of nausea that used to coat his moods.

That trained his self-awareness, since the age of 9. As he sat
through clammy dormitory nights at St. Lebuin, in Deventer, study-
ing Latin   —"becoming bi-lingual like a horse leech"—   by
begrudged candlelight, one clammy hand pressed to an already
capricious 9-year-old stomach. That refused to digest the thrifty
institution food of the Brethren of the Common Life.

—Who "knew no other purpose than the destruction of (their
pupils') natural gifts, with blows, reprimands, & severity, in order
to make the soul fit for monastic life . . ."

For which he felt unfit from the beginning. From which excep-
tional scholarship became his only means of eventual escape.

The memory smell of the food at Deventer still pinches his
narrow nostrils.

It fills Amanda's own nose, suddenly. Polluting the frosted mirror
air with a stench of shame.

Which a whisper chorus of gossip spins into a net, the color of
sin. In which his abandoned mother flails, for 14 years, until she
dies, 2 weeks after the death of her lover. Hurrying into death
after her lover, to recapture the lover who had fled the birth of
his son   from Rotterdam to Gouda   into the shelter of black-
robed penitence.

The memory stench of Gouda, where the son first goes to school.
Amanda feels stung by the keenness of his childhood shame. His
lifelong need to blur the circumstances of his birth.

Of which she knows only what he allowed to be known. The
place: the proud city of Rotterdam. But not the shameful date:
October 27? 1465? 1466? 1467? 1468? 1469???????? Deliberately
obscured, to spite the endlessly spinning whisper chorus, endlessly
commemorating the emerging evidence of illicit love.

Geert Geerts: she shudders with him at the echo of the fatherless name. At the ugly alliteration: Gé Gé gggggggggggggag. Insufficiently muffled by his names of renown: Desiderius Erasmus Roterodamus.

Because his conception was the genius blend of old with young. Which the whisper chorus applauds, when the old is the male, but hisses to death when it is a middle-aged, widowed village-doctor's daughter, reopening her mourning body to a novice priest half her age.

Whose flight from specific fatherhood absolves the son of the commandment: to love and honor his father.

Nor can he love and honor a mother dead of shame. Unless he reinvents her. But the whisper chorus won't let him. Its echo keeps trailing him through black-robed institution corridors, leaving him no choice but to reinvent himself.

Which feels like a form of freedom to Amanda, compared to the mold cast for her by her own enduring mother. Who keeps exacting resemblance tithes from the only daughter. Ignoring the eye shadows & dyed hair   the love affairs   with which Amanda tries to assert her otherness.

—Despite the books Amanda writes. Into which her mother reads proof of their mother-daughter likeness. Which she then explains to Amanda, with a patient smile. Because her mother knows her only daughter better than Amanda can possibly know herself. Because her mother has raised Amanda in her own image. After conceiving Amanda   almost immaculately; without the sin of pleasure   on her wedding night. In full & final payment of her conjugal pledge. Because a legally wedded pregnant woman the mother of a dynasty to be   need not submit to subsequent conjugal sex, lest it hurt the growing seed. Nor does the same young   —not so young; 34-year-old—   nursing mother, lest the sperm curdle her milk.

Her mother's ego image of smiling duty, as limpid as a chilling mountain lake, unrippled by rival images of Amanda's father. Who fled into death, & became a household icon, 1 year & 1 day after Amanda's birth.

When Amanda's mother resumed her interrupted virginity. Smug beneath the widow's robe she had woven for herself, with the unmooring strands of the conjugal cobweb.

—Which looks like a rainbow, hung with dew drops, from the safe retrospection of resumed virginity. From a kneeling position, in front of the icon.

Amanda has never stopped cringing from the moist-pointed kisses her mother affixes —like a stamp!— to the only daughter's turned other cheek. Turned away, not to smell the hunger breath beneath her mother's discreetly cologned demands for love.

Which Amanda vainly tries to find in her heart, for this woman. Who feels less kin to Amanda than other 60-year-olds she meets. This virginal widow, whom she would not go to meet for a second time, if she were not her mother. Whom she would avoid meeting for a first time, at the approach of her robe. Which is warped with duty, & woofed with sacrifice.

The great initial sacrifice of the wedding night, to which her mother submitted. With clenched teeth. Allowing lawful outrage to pierce her 34-year-old privacy, so that Amanda could be conceived.

& incur the debt Amanda cannot pay up as long as her mother lives.

Nor after her mother dies. When her mother's ghost will sit by Amanda's writing elbow, exacting whisper tithes of guilt from the only daughter, instead of the love the only daughter owed her mother, but gave away to men.

—Whisper tithes, as a token of respect for her writing daughter's concentration.

The irony of a daughter of duty, named Amanda   (to refute a dutiful mother's lack of animal tenderness?)   not unlike; & yet so different from   the irony of a son of shame named Desiderius. (By a mother hoping to convince herself   & her native village   of the animal innocence of passion?)

Unless he renamed himself, when he reinvented himself. To sever the emerging scholar from the illegitimate baby, the sickly unwanted boy of his beginnings.

—Which he rewrote   twice   after he became famous, to give a paper reality to his reinventions. 1465? 1466 . . . ?

Or was he hoping to silence the whisper chorus with the learned sound of a Latinized "child of lust"?   —(Lust stands at the top of his list of special remedies for particular vices . . .: flee idleness . . .)

He smiles at her. Probingly; because he, too, recognizes her. Not through a sudden tunnel opening in her mirror, as she recognized him, but rather like a premonition that has come true.

Amanda . . .: he smiles, muttering a Latin greeting with wine-colored lips.

Whose bitter thinness hurts Amanda like the token of a discarded grief. Although her own mouth is full. Heart-shaped; wine-colored with lipstick.

She cannot understand what he is saying, & feels a pang of loss, insufficiently compensated by her deeper knowledge of English.

—Of which he had little need. Even in his correspondence with his English friend Thomas Morus. The easy elegant Latin in which he wrote his thousands of letters   his many books   was understood by all his readers, from London to Rome; to Wittenberg.

Amanda feels nostalgia for the century into which she is peeping, through the hole in her mirror. A century when scholars shared a common language of learning that spanned the barriers of roots   —though not of dogma.

When writers did not outnumber readers.

She strains to remember some of the dead Latin she was taught in school. Which she had absorbed so eagerly, as a 12-year-old.

—"With downright gluttony": according to the round woman with a face like a beaming pancake, who had taught Latin to Amanda; & "religion." Who used to beam down upon Amanda, whose "mind was working like a churn," between 12 & 13. Before the pancake reluctantly rearranged its facial expression, when Amanda's mind became swamped with thoughts of sex.

Which resurface with a blush, preceding random fragments of Latin. Lines from drinking songs, & garbled patriotic quotations.

The unexpected exhortation: *Tu, felix Austria, nube* . . . (a forerunner of: Make love, not war. She can't remember the Latin part about other countries waging wars . . . while happy Austria marries . . .)

Which makes them both laugh. Because Amanda escaped World

War II into an American marriage, & he warned against "the dangers of politically motivated matrimonial alliances," in a short piece called: *The Complaint of Peace.*

Warnings which went unheeded, needless to say: he says to her. Using a wordless language now that speaks directly to her brain. The plight of peace is still the same; as is that of its advocates.

"A free & independent mind which refuses to be bound by any dogma, & declines to join any party, never finds a home upon this earth": he says.

Does Amanda realize that he had to move from Louvain to Basel, because the Catholics accused him of having "laid the egg that Luther hatched." & from Basel to Freibourg   to Besançon-to Basel-to Freibourg; back & forth, during the later part of his life; his "golden" years had been pure lead   because the Lutherans would give him no peace.

Ulrich von Hutten had tracked him down in Basel, & laid siege to his house, when he was refused entry.

A decaying young madman   in his early thirties   burned out with syphilis & Lutheran rage. Whom he had known   & befriended; & encouraged   less than a decade before, when Ulrich had been a flaming young poet; with an astonishingly solid formal education.

—On whose admiringly raised head he had once placed a guilt-iced mentor's hand, in a communion of philosophy & lyricism. The only time his body had surprised him with a stirring of romantic love.

Which the admiring young poet had perhaps sensed   & judged; despite appearances of candor; doubling his mentor's guilt by his seeming unawareness   for the madman to derive a right from the remembered gesture. The license to come pounding on his former mentor's door, in Basel.

Soiling the immaculate Swiss streets with his strident, festering presence.

One afternoon, coming from his printer's workshop, he had found himself walking a few steps behind Ulrich. & had been moved to the marrow by Ulrich's feet: the flaky, glistening marbled purple of the exposed skin. The left foot shoeless, the other on a sole held by a trailing string. The incongruously slender heels, supporting a teetering tent of rags.

Which had exuded a sultry smell of putrefaction.

& then a child had come from the opposite direction. A red-haired girl of 5 or 6, attached to the hand of a woman. Whose arm the girl had raised in a reluctant arc, as she passed Ulrich, & continued to walk with her red head turned backward, following Ulrich's feet with magnetized eyes.

That were much closer to the feet level than his own eyes. Or the stern eyes of the woman.

He had been seized by an impulse then, to touch one of the doubled-over shoulders. To invite Ulrich into his house, to die there in the peace of comfort.

But a man who has spent most of his life appeasing/ignoring a sickly body fears the purplish flaking contact of disease. Of syphilis, when he himself has never transcended the isolation of his skin in shared desire.

Which he is not betraying, therefore, when he retracts the reaching hand. When he retraces his steps, & hurries home by another   longer   route.

Only to find Ulrich lying in the gutter in front of his house. —Amidst a crowd of sparrows, milling about him like roaches, pecking at balls of horse manure.— The feet no longer visible, no longer separate from the malodorous mass.

Around which he tiptoes. Slipping behind his door, like a traitor. —Betrayal as the ultimate detachment.— Closing his shutters on the geyser of invectives that starts spewing from the mass   in a shrill flutter of brown wings   at the sound of his closing door.

Amanda cowers under the avalanche of memories that come rolling over the memory of her own   legitimate; healthy childhood.

That was so different   yet equally unfree, at "home," equally difformative, under the black-robed vigilance of her ever-present mother.

Who also "knew no other purpose than the destruction (of her only daughter's) natural gifts"   —without blows, but with endless reprimands, or sulky severity, in order to make her daughter fit for the widowed life.

From which Amanda keeps trying to elope.

His memories are overlapping hers: She remembers reading a biography of him, which describes him closing his shutters on Ulrich von Hutten   —"betraying Luther's cause for the sake of his lukewarm intellectual comfort."

She must have read the biography during her churning year, between 12 & 13   close to 13, probably   to have provoked a faith riot in her class, with book throwing & rubber band slingshots, when she, who was being raised an acquiescent Protestant, called Luther a hypocrite, an ex-monk who was only trying to justify his marriage to a nun.

To the consternation of the pancake-faced teacher, who had felt compelled to report the incident to Amanda's mother.

Perhaps that was what had switched Amanda's churning mind over to sex: the thought of Luther & his nun making out. To the applause of history. Of biographers, accusing reason of betraying passion.

It still disturbs her. More than it disturbs him. At least at this point. He no longer cares what anyone thinks or says or writes about him.

At this point he would invite Ulrich into his house, & wash the purple feet, & soothe the raging mouth with wine—   to redeem his one furtive gesture of lust & convert it into love.

He wishes that he'd had the courage. For her sake: he says in his wordless language. Raising the pewter mug to his wine-stained smile. Toasting her across 444 years of unchanged humanity.

Does she realize that he, too, had to seek other forms of employment   as a secretary/as a tutor   to support himself & his books. & even then he was forever juggling to maintain a certain quality of life. Out of a certain aesthetic obligation to nature. —Which relied on an alliance with grace, for its reality.

The same aesthetic obligation he felt toward writing. Which requires style as well as content, to be truthful.

For which he was accused of insincerity, by critics who claimed that "true religion had nothing to do with good literature."—As though inarticulateness   grunts & groans   were the criterion of meaning . . .

Amanda nods: She, too, is criticized for being "hung up" on style. Still . . . *He* was world famous . . .

Yes. But she is a woman . . .

She bristles: Is he implying that a woman needs/deserves no recognition for her work? That "a woman is always a fool, no matter what she pretends to be," as he said in the most famous of his books?

That was not *his* opinion. That was Folly, speaking in praise of herself: he says with a touch of impatience.

Which he checks instantly: Was life not simpler for a woman? he asks. Was it not easier to be allowed   expected even   to desire men. Openly; without the subterfuge of mentorship. To be desired by them . . . for her total self. For her body as much as for her mind . . .

Amanda shakes her head. She hasn't found it easy. It's not desirable to be a thinking woman.

The man who saved her from the war by marrying her, resented her thoughts, once he became her husband, & made her cross her legs high at the thigh, to cross them out.

& later lovers were not dissimilar. They wanted her to be a mirror; without reflections of her own. They felt that she was cheating on them, with her writing. & that they had to hurt her, to humiliate her as a woman, to get even with her books.

—Except for one   a sculptor   who loved to listen to her read her work in progress while she posed for him. But physically she was not his type. He liked thin elongated women, whom he could reconstruct in wire. Whereas for her, he's felt obliged to work in stone . . .

He had not always been painted to his liking either: he tells her with pointed lips: & never by a lover. But then, there had not been much to like about his looks; except for the saving grace of clothes . . .

She feels that she is disappointing him. As though her healthy female body had been his gift to her. A thoughtful   perhaps costly   birthday present, for which he expected to be thanked.

She wants to tell him that: Yes! She's grateful. Happy to lead a woman's life.

That she has found a total love now. A flaming young poet with an astonishingly solid formal education, who desires her completely, body books & soul.

But he can read her eyes. & see her poet's eyes in them, liquid with desire for mentorship   & subsequent publication   when they make love.

He starts receding   fading with disappointment   growing dimmer; dustier.

The tunnel in her mirror narrows, tightening like a strep throat. Which yields a final wordless plea: To answer her ringing doorbell. Not to fail to take Ulrich in at last.

Amanda expects to see her poet lover through the peephole in her apartment door. But it is her mother she sees, magnified into a huge black widow, pressing the bell with 8 hairy legs.

SIX POEMS

GUILLEVIC

Translated from the French by Dori Katz

ELEGIES

There will always be a light
Unlike any other
That could be the place.

There will always be
No reason to stop.

Always
No reason to know why.

There will always be
A good light to encounter,
The one

Where you have nothing more to lose.

•

Took some sand in his hands
Did not know
Whom to give it to.

Yes, it happened
By sunset.

Yes, it was at the edge
Of the ocean.

What
Difference does it make?

•

Neither sky, nor clouds
Nor stones, nor leaves,
Not even the wind

Know anything of your story
When you ask.

Go on nevertheless
Go on
Bearing it.

•

I must have been statue,

Before being this man
Reiterating the dark and not liking to move.

I must have stayed polished stone for a long time,
Hardly aware of being looked at, exposed
And continuing its stone equation.

Left in my stoniness
To more twistings than in the air,

And willing to accept
A cramped life.

•

Your death
Is in the long run only

A stroke of an eraser
That didn't connect.

And yet
It's with it, it's in it

That you drink this glass and watch
The tree dying more slowly.

     •

No fire
On the heath and no one
In the night.

This laughter around you.

The house, nor the woman
Were there, but space.

—Later, later,
You'll be able to live it.

     •

It was at the edge of clouds.

Towards the bottom of clouds,
In their underparts,

Very low
Near the earth.

There must have been somewhere
Pieces of time suffering,

Pools of time
Unused.

·

If you were not a thing
Like things are,

Embrangled,
Twisted like them,

Whirled, carrying
Whirlwinds away,

If you were not, also, fed
By galaxies, by burnings,

—Then,
The two of us,
Why?

·

When
Will the fog dissipate

The weight things have
On each other?

And the balance be clear
Between the white and the raw,
Between the sun and the knife,
Between the sea and my lap,

Between your dream and me
Turned towards you.

When will I lie down
At pleasure, in your sleep?

When will the rainbow come
To stabilize my hand?

When will we go motionless
There where motion will detain us,

In the middle
Interminably present

Of the break
And equilibrium?

ENCOUNTER

So:

A gray stone

Just big enough
To be held
Easily in hand.

Irregular, with
Angles, roundness.

Granite rather
Than not.

Drawn from a time
It had only itself
As company.

    •

Gray stone,
Stroked both
By fingers and sun.

Light
Always just emerging.

.

Comes a long rest
Stop of time
And movement.

All misfortunes as though hanging
Avoidable.

The universe suspended
Still and set on a curved path.

WHEN

I
When just before noon
The sun is on the prairie

And the heat
Is good, according to daisies,
On a par with flowers
On a par with roots

And the meadow is open
To fields, to moors,
To roads, to sky,

There is:
A song that is as much silence,

And all things
Have time to look at each other,

The blade of grass
Measures the world.

II
When many things
Yield under the sun,

When you don't want
To leave the field, the embankment,

When you feel in collusion
With all the greens,

With the gate and further on
The roofs of the hamlet,

You are tempted to say
That all over, the globe
Is being accomplished.

III
When towards evening the beach
Is the color of the sea,

And the sea
Is only the extension of the beach,

When nothing is sure
But this grayness which isn't even gray

This horizontal setting and above
Vague, translucid, the hemisphere,

You must quit
This kind of endlessness.

IV
When the sea left
Some seaweed on the sand

And a tern flies by
Breaking away from the cliffs,

When the horizon
Is blurred with mist,
Anticipating the sun—

The sea's breath
Opens doors,

Makes the foundations from before
Long ago, shift

The ones you feel
In every heave

The ones we have
Our rooms in forever,

For this forever in us
Like the ocean.

V
When the sky
Has no outward
Look,

And life
Goes on nevertheless
As though nothing happened,

And you offer me the glass of.wine
Looking at my face
While looking at the glass—

We would be happy
For a bit of blue.

But your domain
Has no limits.

This dim sky
Is only a moment

In the passing
Of one to the other.

We have kept
Oceans that are opaque.

From time to time
They burn us.

VI
When somewhere a body
Is being tortured that cannot
Scream louder than itself

Nothing mentions it.
The ground

Is like another day
The air also, the leaves,
The curves, the colors
And the barking of a dog
At the borders of the Beauce.

But it's a fact,
Torturing goes on every day
From time immemorial,

The habit took hold,
And it's being recorded
With no great variation.

THE CHARNEL HOUSES

Walk among the flowers and look:
At the end of the field, the charnel house.

Not more than a hundred of them but in a pile,
A small giant insect belly
With feet sticking out everywhere.

You can tell their gender by their shoes.
Their eyes probably drowned.

—They also
Preferred flowers.

•

At one side of the charnel house
Slightly raised, venturesome,

A leg—a woman's leg
Of course—

A young leg
With a black stocking

And a thigh
A real thigh,

Young—and nothing,
Nothing.

•

Their underwear is not
What rots first,

You can see bits of it, over there,
Calcified by matter

Looking like exposed
Pieces of flesh still hanging on.

How many knew why
How many died knowing,
How many didn't know what?

Those who wept,
Their eyes are all alike,

Holes in bones
Or lead melting.

.

They said yes
To rotting.

They agreed,
They left us.

We have nothing to do
With their rotting.

.

We're going to sort them out,
As much as possible,

Put each one
In his own pit,

Because together
They make too much silence against noise.

.

If it weren't absolutely
Impossible,

You would say a woman
Drunk with love-making
Falling asleep.

        •

If the mouth is open,
Or whatever is left of it,

It's probably because they sang,
Screamed triumphantly,

Or because their jaws
Dropped in fear

—Maybe by accident,
And some soil got in.

        •

There are places you can't tell
If it's clay or if it's flesh

And you're afraid that all over
The earth might be like that, and stick.

        •

If only they would become
Skeletons right away

As clean and hard
As real skeletons

And not this mixture
With mud.

        •

Who among us
Would lie down with them

For an hour, for an hour or two
Just as homage.

•

Where is the wound
Answering?

Where is the wound
On living bodies?

Where is the wound—
So we can see it,

Can heal it.

•

Here
Does not lie

Here or there, will never
Lie

What remains
What will remain
Of those bodies.

PORTRAITS

To Jean Paulhan

A handsome draft horse
As companion
He traveled a long time
And crossed many countries.

Disgrace was meaningless
And meaningless the great snubs
Encountered in plains,

For at night he slept
In some parade
Lying against the beast,

And they were in love
From flesh to flesh
In all lands.

But one night when
The sun was not
Redder than often,

The horse bit him
In the hand stroking

While his eye
Was open and calm
And perhaps seeing.

•

Once he had looked at all the monsters close up
And seen they were all made of the same fiber,

He could sit reassured in a bright room
And see space.

•

He shook before lights
He shook before small branches.

He didn't like windows
He didn't trust birds.

He couldn't
Be anymore.

    •

Yet when it was clear
That the city was burning
In the crash of bombs,

He dared for once
Be on first name basis
With things he touched
On the table and the walls.

    •

Speaking to the doll
Whose eyes recalled
Those he couldn't find

And whose outstretched arms
Had been broken
By him, some other evening.

    •

Since crime was too strong a taste for him
And yet destruction his great need

He had to fill his days willy-nilly
Creating emptiness around him with his eyes.

    •

Stretched out on mossy ground and seeing the day
Would not be duplicated

He dreamed that wounded, hands touched
Then washed him with water flowing from the rock.

MAGNIFICAT

1
I kiss your knees.
I come.

2
Glorious
This trembling

On the point
Of approaching.

3
Your lip.

One,
The other.

4
To think
There are times

When for you
I am

Lighter than air.

5
Only then,

Has the horizon
Disappeared.

The middle is everywhere—
And I'm in it.

6
In you

The world is summed up
With no reduction.

7
Your smell, leafmold,

Has crossed seas
Full of bacteria.

8
You tell
The swelling of seas

On their way
To being calmed.

9
In you, I am
A proxy—

Of what?

10
One of your voices
Reaches me

Through these waters crossed
Before the era of speech.

11
The tides,
The sliding of rocks,
The flight of seagulls

Fill your contours
For my use.

12
This rhythmic crawling
Towards the horizonless kingdom.

13
The boldness

To give our bodies

What we knew
More gaping

Than any
Definition.

14
Like lava
Crawling under the ground
Gathering,

Reaching the opening,
Yielding,

Making room
For more lava.

15
Of these tendernesses
That make you scream.

16
Passage cleared,
Always to be cleared again

Towards the starting point
Towards its thrust

Its explosion.

17
Like the Gulf Stream

Crossing
The oceans

That asked for it.

18
I fall back
Out of you,

Out of the empire
That has your door.

19
You let me
Come in.

You kept me long enough
To live through

What this body can
Believing itself exiled.

20
It knows
Your body

How the molecules
Emerge into petals

Into what comes up trembling
Till the edge of your eyes.

21
I see you
I don't see you

In a half-light
On the instance of volcano.

22
A way
of paying homage

To the undefinable
Spurring us on.

23
Now, no one

Needs
To want to be God.

24
Previously
For depths long,

We trudged

Through fits of impatience
Of salt and iodide.

25
For that
The time is always right.

26
The only way
I know

Of diving deeply
Into prehistory.

27
Geometric premise
Of cohesion

Between us
And the magma.

28
Slide
Into the canticle's

Cavern
Of self devise.

29
What we near
What we touch

Shows us yet
Another beyond

To cross
To caress.

30
My continent.

My ocean
Of continents.

31
Respite
Was not for us.

Motion
Is our stopping place.

32
How to be closer yet
Being inside?

33
Eternity

Is an open space,

A point
Of self-confinement.

34
We taught
Each other
What it is.

35
There are no birds
More hawk than us.

36
It's really you.

These are the true details
Of your face.

There are times
I recognize you

From the inside
Of your empire.

37
So, the present,
The past, the future

Can weave
The same moment

Into a space
Between spaces.

38
Let's try living for a long time
Further than ourselves.

39
Our advance

Occurs in a dark
Fringed with light,
More or less.

40
Time
Immeasurable

Full
Of immemorial events

In the today
Of the immediate.

41
That my hands feel you.
That I know it.

42
Here
Leaving and not leaving

Are defined
In the infinite tangential,

In the hand to hand.

43
An island. An island

Seaweed
To cling to.

An island
A foothold.

44
Venturing in you
Its borders.

Never
Hopeless.

45
Joined for a long time
Our lips act out

The fever of rocks
Those not emerging.

46
Deliver me
Of this delirium

Of which I am
Never delivered.

47
Our breathlessness
Is the tide's

Is the sun's
Towards his most brilliant.

Is the night's
When daylight threatens.

48
Are you very sure

Not to have slept
Outside your body

In this long moment

Where memory is
Sometimes erased?

49
Stay. Stay.

Don't always leave
Even right next to me,

With the winds, with the rivers
With all the currents
Ploughing the earth.

Stay like this, a woman's
Body comfortable in a bed.

50
Go through the motions
Of daily life again.

Be this body
Returning

Harvested, awaiting
The gathering moment.

51
We'll have much time to be
No more than we are

Caressing our boundaries.

52
Perhaps
One never returns,

One stays
For days,

A flesh equation
Bearer of breakthroughs
That make plants grow.

INTERVIEW WITH SAMUEL ASTONGUET

ALAIN NADAUD

Translated from the French by Breon Mitchell

(Transcription of an interview by Alain Nadaud with Samuel Astonguet at the latter's home)

ALAIN NADAUD—Samuel Astonguet, you've been living in retirement for several years now, without publishing anything . . .

SAMUEL ASTONGUET—(. . .)

A.N.—There's been a good deal of curiosity about your silence. Pierre Rasque, whose commentaries continue to illuminate your works, stated again quite recently that you ceased writing upon your return from a trip you made to India in 1965, at least if his information is accurate . . .

SAMUEL ASTONGUET—It's accurate.

A.N.—The critics are unanimous in considering you a great writer. And we're all familiar with the numerous and very strange short stories you've written about India. Why is it then that you ceased writing after that voyage? What happened? Were you disappointed? Subjected to special pressures? Could you say a few words about that trip?

SAMUEL ASTONGUET—Certainly, and since it's become common knowledge, I no longer have any reason to hide it from you. I arrived in Bombay in June of '65; it was a rainy morning. Immobilized for an instant at the top of the steps from the airplane,

I was struck immediately by the violence of the wind, a hot wind, yet completely saturated with rain. I remember that we had to cross an open space to the terminal on foot without being able to walk anywhere but through puddles of water; from that moment on my feet were soaked, and they remained that way practically throughout my stay. As one of the customs officers was going through my luggage, I recognized Apasari Satchinadam, pressed against the railing by the crowd . . .

A.N.—Apasari Satchinadam? Didn't you sign that name to your very first stories?

SAMUEL ASTONGUET—Yes, indeed. You have a good memory. Short and stocky, dressed in the European manner, his thin hair plastered obstinately to his forehead by the wind, he waited for me, impassive as always, making only the slightest sign to me with the rolled-up newspaper in his hand.

A.N.—Excuse me for interrupting, but there's a point concerning Apasari Satchinadam which we might be able to clear up before going any further . . .

SAMUEL ASTONGUET—Yes, but not right now! Let me go on, please. I'll come back to that . . . As soon as I had passed through the final police controls, Apasari Satchinadam took the suitcase from me and conducted me into a small yellow-and-black taxi which took us directly to his home. It was in the quarter called Mahim, if I'm not mistaken. He lived not far from the beach, on the ground floor of a small apartment building with a gray-and-white façade which had been completely washed out by the rains. I seem to be losing myself in unimportant details, but believe me, it's essential, I have to remember everything exactly as it was. Through the window you could see the coconut trees twisting in the wind; the air was sultry, now and again it would rain abruptly, the monsoon was raging that year in Bombay.

A.N.—You already knew the city, didn't you?

SAMUEL ASTONGUET—Yes, of course! I spent my whole childhood there with my parents. That's where I learned Marathi. To tell the truth, the city hadn't changed much. I found again, with infinite pleasure, "Marine Drive" running along the bay, and, on the other side, "The Gateway of India," its docks battered furiously by the sea; and everywhere those large crows, so popular in Bombay, whose temerity has never ceased to astonish me. When

I was with Apasari Satchinadam, even though we had a lot we might have said to one another, we usually preferred to drink a few beers in silence at the "Volga" or beside the Flora Fountain.

A.N.—It seems strange to me that you keep evoking the name of Apasari Satchinadam, and reveal that he's a real person. We're used to viewing his name simply as an assumed one. Now that you've affirmed his existence, what relationship does he have to your own works?

SAMUEL ASTONGUET—In fact, I had known Apasari Satchinadam for a long time, ever since a symposium in London devoted to Indian literature. I was tied up with other affairs, and unfortunately had to miss his paper, but according to my colleagues, his lecture would have been remarkable if it hadn't been inaudible. A technical difficulty—a high-pitched tone in the earphones—had in fact effaced the major portion of his presentation. As a last resort, just before he left again for Bombay, he gave me his notes, which I subsequently published in a specialized journal. They concerned, if I remember correctly, the influence of the "Brihadaranyaka Upanishad" upon recent tendencies in Marathi literature.

A.N.—To return to your own stories, you only used the name Apasari Satchinadam then as a pseudonym, out of modesty perhaps, or to lend an air of probability to your stories?

SAMUEL ASTONGUET—Not altogether: Apasari Satchinadam actually was a writer. When I knew him, he had already published a volume of poems in Bombay and a few short stories in Calcutta and the United States. In fact, at the conclusion of the symposium, and before he had taken the plane back to his country, I asked him to send me a few of his texts in Marathi, which I proposed to translate directly into French. He did so in the following months; and his stories, to tell the truth, left me stupefied.

A.N.—Were you already writing yourself at that period?

SAMUEL ASTONGUET—Yes, short stories. I had also published a few of them in second-rate journals. But the texts of Apasari Satchinadam far surpassed them in logic and quality. First of all, most of them related events so precise it seemed that I had lived them myself, as one sometimes feels in listening to an ancient chronicle; moreover, the rhythm and the tone of his stories were so intimate and familiar to me that I had the impression of talking to myself when I was reading them. To be perfectly frank, in contact with them I felt a sentiment at once of malaise and passion, similar to the feeling one has with texts one is jealous of not having written, but a feeling as well that they had been stolen from me. Of course, and although they were very simply written, dangerous even for that reason, I could not, except to admit that they called forth in me a sort of resentment, accuse them of anything more, for they treated events of little importance; but events which, seen from a certain perspective, opened themselves to multiple layers of reading which, you may easily imagine, lent to the whole a dimension one was far from suspecting at the beginning. Worse, the immobile violence which emanated from them at times cut off the sources of my own inspiration. I don't know if you understand me; caught in the game, touched to the quick, I stopped writing for myself and settled down to the translation of his admirable stories. From time to time I would write to Apasari Satchinadam to keep him informed of the state of my labors, and he, while thanking me, would continue to send me other stories from Bombay.

A.N.—So you really did translate the stories of Apasari Satchinadam from the Marathi into French? Have they been published? How does one tell them from your own? I must admit I don't quite understand how . . .

SAMUEL ASTONGUET—Indeed, it's impossible. No sooner were they translated, and with an ease which at first disconcerted me, than they were published and attained immediate success, first in France and then in Europe. Strangely enough as well, certain of my colleagues to whom I had first shown the texts in Marathi, and who judged them of little significance, found themselves among the most enthusiastic admirers. My translations, they wrote in their articles, presented these stories in a new light, and, by a change of angle in the illumination, threw them into a relief which revealed both a coherence and a complexity which the original text, on first encounter, did not display. Was it the passage from one language to another which thus gave value to certain hidden elements? The change of perspective which unveiled an architecture which until then had remained secret? In any case their success was such that a journal wished to devote a special issue to them, and asked me to compose a short introduction for it.

A.N.—This is a whole area of your activity which has remained almost unknown to the public. Still it seems that a considerable confusion has thus arisen between this Indian author and you, a confusion to which, up to now, you have not set any precise limits. Is that intentional?

SAMUEL ASTONGUET—A confusion which is inherent in all attempts at translation . . .

A.N.—Yes, but a confusion which you foster and to which you seem attached. If not, why haven't you refuted the essay published by Pierre Rasque which affirms, on the basis of textual evidence, precisely that Apasari Satchinadam never really existed, is nothing but a pure fiction?

SAMUEL ASTONGUET—That's got nothing to do with it! Anyway, Pierre Rasque can publish what he wants.

A.N.—And this trip to India that you began telling us about just a while ago, did you really go there, or was it just a dream? Once and for all, to which realm does Apasari Satchinadam belong?

SAMUEL ASTONGUET—(Breaks out laughing) That's just the point, the last day we spent in Bombay, Apasari Satchinadam kept reminding me, with a smile which at first I found not at all ambiguous, of our years of collaboration, from text to text, from one language to the other, with all that borderland of uncertainty, that blurred area which is generated by such an interaction. And it was, as in your case, toward this undefined zone, this fundamental imprecision in which all translation attempts to articulate itself, that his questions led. There existed between us, in those places where the texts did not exactly coincide, in the blank spaces between the words, an inviolate zone, a no man's land, which neither one of us could penetrate. And beyond this dividing line, each betrayal became a possibility, if not a foregone conclusion.

A.N.—You would speak openly of them?

SAMUEL ASTONGUET—No, just guardedly, but that was just about the only thing we talked about during the interminable journey by train which, starting in Bombay, was to allow us to travel across the Indian subcontinent in all directions over several months. Not that it was a tourist trip, far from it! Since then, by the way, I've forgotten the order of the stages of our journey; place names, locales, dates, everything's a bit confused in my memory. The first thing he wanted to show me, strangely enough, were the settings where certain of his short stories were supposed to have taken place. He had already started in Bombay moreover:

"You remember," he said to me, "in one of my stories, the scene at the cemetery near the beach, where a huge concrete sewage pipe pours its filth into the sea; well look, this is the place."

It was raining. I looked at the beach and the blackish trail from the sewage pipe which extended far into the sea. I was thus confronted by the real place which had served as the setting for his story, as if I were serving as a witness to the truth of that which he had written. At first, and without being annoyed by it, I thought that he was trying to deepen my knowledge of India, perhaps in order to help me in translating his texts.

A.N.—Isn't what you have described the scene in "Les Funérailles de Raja,"[1] a short story, which, however, was attributed to you at the time?

SAMUEL ASTONGUET—Yes, that's the one! But is it really my fault if the critics have been so insistent about attributing to me the authorship of a work which I did nothing but translate? In fact, however, the confusion becomes even greater in the case of another story which takes place in Mahabalipuram, perhaps a hundred kilometers south of Madras.

A.N.—A place which you visited as well, in the company of your friend?

SAMUEL ASTONGUET—Yes, of course! And I remember even more clearly that it was there that I began to understand the subtle game which Apasari Satchinadam was playing. After having left our things at a shabby hotel, we cut back across country to the sea. There we wound up at a small bay in which the waves were very strong. Since we had walked a long way, we sat down upon the grass:

"You haven't forgotten, in another story, the meeting between Milinda and the Brahmin; well here's where it took place. And a little further down the way, just by those temples, is where Milinda drowned."

Then he told me about the neighboring temples, erected right on the beach, some of which, according to legend, had since been

[1] Les Funérailles de Raja. Editions du Cerf-volant, Paris 1961

covered by water. Apasari Satchinadam's gaze, dark behind his large glasses, was fixed upon me as if awaiting some gesture or response. At that moment something stirred within me. I remembered the story very well, and to the best of my recollection (try as hard as I could to recall the contrary), I had never made the connection with these "sea-side temples." How, unless I was unaware of their existence, could I have forgotten the ones thought to have been engulfed? I could not help admitting to myself that precisely this oversight falsified the whole sense of my translation, the wording of which I recalled quite clearly. What I had taken for a more or less symbolic metaphor in the title was nothing other than a self-evident reality. As if seized by doubt, I asked Apasari Satchinadam to take me to these famous temples. This was, it should be noted, the only time that he allowed me to verify something for myself, and to touch with my hand the reality which had escaped me. On other occasions this had only been implicit. I was truly nonplussed: the temples of black sandstone rose up at the very edge of the waves, their corners worn and polished by the steady wind from the gulf of Bengal, saturated with sand and spray. Scarcely having realized my error, for a moment I might even have recognized beneath the water the far and indistinct outline of the vanished temples. I was already mentally at work on the revisions which I would hasten to make in my translation upon returning to Paris.

A.N.—Didn't you tell me a few minutes ago that it was thanks precisely to "Temple sous les eaux"[2] that you became first known, and then famous?

SAMUEL ASTONGUET—Yes, although it's a little more complicated than that. But it's true that it was after this story that René Hatman, my editor, definitely stopped believing in the existence of Apasari Satchinadam. Previously, he hadn't known what to believe. The story was soon to appear as part of a volume, and it seems it had become evident that the following fall the works of Apasari Satchinadam—a dozen texts in all—would be crowned with a literary prize. For this occasion, René Hatman—was it duplicity on his part?—asked me to convey an invitation to the

[2] "Le temple sous les eaux" in œuvres complètes, t. II. Editions la Porte Ouverte, Paris.

author to come to France. Far from issuing this invitation, I waited a few weeks and reported, with a knowing air, that he had no intention of coming. In the end the prize was awarded to someone else.

A.N.—It was then, wasn't it, that the name of Apasari Satchinadam disappeared from that editor's catalogue, since it had become clear to everyone that under the cover of your work as a translator, you were in fact the sole author of these stories . . .

SAMUEL ASTONGUET—Yes, since no one had the least evidence of his existence. I was both his translator and his sole intermediary. No one really knew him or had his address. From the moment that a possible hoax seemed to have been discovered, no one cared to believe in the existence of this supposed Indian author. It must be said that I didn't make the slightest attempt to lessen the ambiguity or dispel the doubt. The more so since the first commentaries of Pierre Rasque on these texts began to call forth a lively public interest in them.

A.N.—That's all very surprising on your part, and overturns all our ideas about you. I remain floored by it . . . But didn't Apasari Satchinadam ever learn of your machinations? Didn't he ever let you know about it? After all, you'll allow me to express some degree of reserve with regard to your intellectual honesty. Are we justified, in your opinion, in considering you anything other than a vulgar plagiarist?

SAMUEL ASTONGUET—I accept that analysis. It's even worse than that, as you'll soon see, if we are fortunate enough to come to the end of this story. But after all, what recourse did he have? As for knowing whether he was aware of it or not, that's the question I was always asking myself. Even when I received his letter inviting me to come to India, I couldn't tell. I wasn't distrustful. It was only after several weeks of the journey with him that I gradually become certain that he knew, by some means or other, of the contents of my translations. I remember quite well how I came to realize it: it was in the course of our trip to Jamshedpur that I began to feel uneasy, and to discover in the journey a logic which led me to suppose that Apasari Satchinadam knew.

In the middle of the night we descended from the train onto the deserted platform of some lonely station a few kilometers outside of Jamshedpur, in its suburbs in fact. We awaited daybreak seated upon the baggage wagons, and as soon as it was light enough, we entered into the streets of the town. I was beginning to get very tired, and since we seemed to have a good distance to go, I talked my friend into taking a rickshaw. It soon deposited us before a large gray ramshackle house, slightly dilapidated, with permanently illuminated neon lights on the terrace of each floor:

"Surely you haven't forgotten the description of the offices of the company where Samatha was employed in my short story called 'The Hall of the Archives'? Apasari Satchinadam asked me in a low voice. "Well, here we are! I once worked here myself in days gone by. Come on!"

Without waiting, he had the caretaker unbolt the door and then preceded me into the halls. The workers hadn't arrived yet, and everything had been left in an indescribable disorder from the night before. Unless the workers themselves had quit the place long ago. Everywhere, in the dust, there were piles of dossiers, bundles of documents tied up with string, papers blown to the floor by the night wind in every corner. The story I had translated came back to me in its slightest details. Suddenly the arrangement of the rooms, different on every floor, struck me, and it would have been very hard not to make the connection with the overall plan of his story, which made implicit reference to it, as if having traced from it its very structure. You see, all this may seem a bit complicated at first, but the fact is that, in light of the floor plan, one saw immediately why the protagonist refused the promotion which would have led him to change offices, and provoked in consequence the death of the person who was to have replaced him: indeed the backstairs from the last terrace had no banister. I don't know if you remember the whole of that story but I for one haven't forgotten any of it. At that period, unfortunately, I didn't know the terrible game that Apasari Satchinadam had given himself over to with regard to certain material details which at first seemed quite insignificant. At the same time I was unaware, to the extent that it was barely suggested, of the hostility which emanated from certain objects, a hostility contained in the words, almost in the way itself in which these objects were presented and described in the text. Indeed, the menace which the employees of the company felt pressing in upon them grew precisely within the text of the story itself, more explicitly, in the progression and effect of the wording of its description. A secret and unbearable menace which posed completely different questions, you realize, than the simple quasi-detective story to which—in spite of all its richness—I had so miserably reduced it.

A.N.—Did Apasari Satchinadam know French?

SAMUEL ASTONGUET—To tell the truth I never knew. But it was the look he gave me when we returned to the station that made me doubt the naïveté of his intentions. We had already covered thousands of kilometers by train at the moment when I realized that each stage of the journey brought me face to face with a new defeat. Of all that he had written, of everything that I had appropriated as my own in the act of translation, I had, for all practical purposes, grasped nothing. On the contrary, and in spite of all my errors, his works seemed to me as if they were new and practically intact. I suggested to him that we end the journey at that point and return: he didn't question the decision. Without saying anything about it, he had allowed me to discover, over the course of the weeks, that there might have been certain facts which had escaped me, and which could be the source of certain misformulations, if not inexactitudes, which had slipped into my translations. "You see," he seemed to insinuate, "you've translated this phrase like that; now that's not at all accurate, it's supposed to also mean this. You know in India everything has two faces, signifying at once a thing and its contrary." I made no attempt to defend myself. Besides, I was worn out. The voyage which we had undertaken had taken on, from time to time, the appearance of a dream. We had traveled under the worst conditions. We would pass entire nights sitting on the ground at railway platforms where no train ever seemed to pass. We would sometimes sleep in the first-class waiting rooms, stretched out uncomfortably on tables or benches, but most often curled up against one another in huge halls, near to the ticket windows where the crowd of travelers, porters, and beggars jostled one another. At mealtimes we would head for one of the small smelly restaurants which bordered the station. Then, after hours and days, the train would be announced. We would hurry along the platform to get there ahead of the train. Scarcely had the locomotive, puffing steam, entered the station, when, amid the general precipitation, we would clutch at the steps of the cars like all the others in order to hurl ourselves into the already over-filled compartments, only too happy to be able to seat ourselves again on our luggage in the aisles. Then we would remain there for hours, immobilized for no apparent reason in the overpowering damp heat, and by the time the train finally pulled out, we would already be exhausted.

A.N.—Did you ever fall ill?

SAMUEL ASTONGUET—Yes, many times: diarrhea, malaria, vomiting; I couldn't keep anything down, everything nauseated me; I lost a lot of weight. When I became seriously ill, Apasari Satchinadam placed me in the care of one of his friends—he had acquaintances in almost every city in India—and only returned to get me later.

One day we returned to Benares. I had been at my sickest there, eating nothing but bitter oranges and tea. Seated before me, Apasari Satchinadam said nothing. At the most he took off his glasses now and then and simply wiped them on a fold of his shirt. We had traveled all night perched on the wooden luggage racks, almost without sleeping. At every stop a crowd of people would get off and on, arguing over the seats. I don't know if it was a dream or reality, but it seemed to me, in my half-sleep, that we had remained stationary on a side track for a good part of the night. All the while the cries of the platform merchants were echoing, again and again: the cry as from beyond the grave, serious and slow, of the tea merchant:

"Chai! . . . Chai! . . ."

and in sharper tone, the shrill voice of another merchant cutting quickly cross the first:

"Coffee! Coffee! Coffee!"

Now day was dawning and the train rolled along slowly through open country, winding across the rice fields. All the cars were empty. The floor was covered with various forms of refuse, scraps and cigarette butts. Suddenly I had the feeling that Apasari Satchinadam was trying to disorient me, to make me lose time, to cut me off from my bases. Had we been traveling about, haphazardly, constantly retracing our steps, and spending all that money, just to see one of the sewer pipes of Bombay, the market-place at Cochin, the port of Calcutta, a suburb of Jamshedpur, the park at Hyderabad, and others I haven't even mentioned to you, simply because those places were the fictitious settings in which his stories took place? Was it in order to confront me with their own truth and to oblige me to measure the distance which separated me from them, to understand the reason why they would always remain foreign to me? Was there not in this voyage, as if traced in filigree, a long-sensed menace, growing sharper and sharper, pointing toward my own obvious demise? A voyage which seemed to have no other goal than to make me lose face, to humiliate me, and little by little to cause me to founder in the belly of the subcontinent where, by dint of privations, and at the end of my strengh, I would end by disappearing and dying. Was not Apasari Satchinadam taking his revenge in this way, was he not attempting, without in the least betraying his intention, to bring about my proper destruction, after having already succeeded in losing me in the labyrinth of his texts, of which, I must admit, I never understood anything at all, and which, at that moment, were closing behind me like a trap, seemingly compact and inpenetrable. Caught in a snare formed by the convergence of incertitude, fatigue, and nausea, I was suddenly seized by a panic-stricken impulse, a last involuntary reflex, to struggle.

As the train slowed down again, I acted as if I were getting up to go to the window, then, turning around suddenly, I threw myself upon Apasari Satchinadam. We rolled about beneath the seat in the dust and the garbage, but he couldn't tear my fingers from their hold around his throat. When he finally ceased struggling, his face twisted in a strange grimace, I pushed him underneath the bench as far as I could with my foot. I was in a sweat. I felt slightly giddy and the blood was pounding in my temples. I picked up my bag and, standing on the steps of the car, I waited for the train to lose a little speed before jumping onto the ballast . . .

I wasn't far from Kanpur. I arrived there on foot. I decided to take the bus from there to New Delhi. It was market day; there was a large crowd. I bought my ticket in advance and went to sit in the rear next to a window. Just as the bus was maneuvering in reverse to get back onto the blacktop road, I had something like a hallucination: for a fraction of a second, I thought I saw Apasari Satchinadam gazing fixedly at me through the crowd.

There, now you know the whole story. If you would be so kind as to allow me to be myself now, I would greatly appreciate it. Au revoir, monsieur.

A few days after this interview, we learned that Samuel Astonguet had been killed in an accident. This was thus his last public utterance. It is in his honor, and after a good deal of hesitation, that we have decided to publish this interview, strange as it may be in many respects. In spite of all our attempts, we have been unable to find, in his papers or in his correspondence, the least trace of the existence of Apasari Satchinadam. Moreover, to our great astonishment, one of his friends has assured us that Samuel Astonguet never knew a word of Marathi; and no visa for India appears in his passport during the period under discussion.

We all appreciate the talent and imagination of Samuel Astonguet, but we may never know whether, in breaking his silence, he felt obliged to offer this ultimate terrible confession, or whether, taking up once more the thread of his former tales, he simply presented us with the last of all his stories.

FOUR POEMS

RUTH DOMINO

Translated from the Italian by Daniel Hoffman and Jerre Mangione

BIRCH TREE

Stone under foot
Little owl in its hair
Dew on breast
My birch tree
Unrivaled

An evening breath
Shudder scarce born
Already spent among leaves
Unrivaled
Without heart, the pain

STREET OF SHELLS

Every step
a shell
a small tongue

speaking in the wind's breath
with a thousand voices
of sand.
They, too, the refugees
from drowned frontiers.

Every step
a shell
a small fear
a gem furrowed by howling
when the werewolf
hunted among a thousand dreams.
They, too,
petrified leaves.

I have walked too much
in the charnel house of shells.
Foot's old leather
feels no longer.
Nor gilded agony
of gnat in amber
when the tree of life
cracked and fell; it, too,
a lost roar.

BALLAD OF THE DAY

Was it yesterday or was today the day
when the raven drank slow tears
that tolled the curfew, and the shadow writing
on the plain of snow?

Was the day another yesterday when singing
black upon the gibbet, raven flew
from the crematories, drunk
on the smoke and writing

the deaths of brothers on the snow?

Never! they reply.—The smoke
never wrote the black
song of drunken raven
on the plain. Never, neither

yesterday, nor other yesterday!
Do you hear the cry that cleaves
slow tears of the bell
tolling the brothers' deaths? O, no,

they answer, no, it is the shadow
of the evening writes across the plain
smudge on snow
the hour, as always.

MOMENTS

1
In a rock, enormous, seated,
a wrinkle.
A wrinkle in the flesh
on a minuscule
vein beneath the wind's caress.
In that moment
hanging from the tree
the worm, nibbling
in the apple's dream,
stops.

2
I held the apple's face,
a little sucking sun
between my hands,

then between my deadly
teeth—in that
instant
delight's brief dream
dies, without destination.

3
It was the time of bees,
the last word
fastened
on the flowered flesh—
in an instant
the mediator's heart
stops—Ah, the gift
of immortality
which, as a rule,
is humorless.

THE COLDEST YEAR OF GRACE

GIOVANNI RABONI

Translated from the Italian by Vinio Rossi and Stuart Friebert

1
The feet that we don't have—
the felt boots that have been stolen from us
bring us to the snowy marketplace one morning
to sell turtledoves and rabbits
put together the little cages from stakes
to hide the Siberian cats
in their own fur, half closed like a wound.

2
Another life,
our friend with his heavy beard, the shy eyeglasses
raises with joy
the fish by the tail
offers it baked to us, or boiled while
he unwraps it from the newspapers
as if it were night or morning, and nothing raw
were to separate us.

3
From the numbers, from two numbers, now, you try to understand:
the three albino lion cubs

born yesterday in Australia,
your daughter's albino cat
found dead beneath a tree this morning, in the garden:
those of a short life, they say—this one assassinated.
You give yourself things to do, you multiply, divide
white by white, threat by misfortune.

4
Once, on the steps, the other time
at a kitchen table
sensing you unthreading life
perhaps (I think of it now) it was
Giorgi and Marzia's death you were seeking, trying
to swallow it, spit it out, trying to psychosomaticize it,
robbing it from the future
in two far-off houses . . .

5
It happened once, it happens to me
in dreams sometimes
from the smoke-covered Franz Joseph
to the great windows of the Südbahnhof
snowed-in city-stretch
impossible coincidence
in the twilight thick with street lamps
before the force of day breaks, forever.

6
We have friends who take us
to the most famous beer halls,
the waiters going round and round, counting the mugs,
swans, saints, or lions—
there's no better place in Europe, no warmer, to taste
the gray of midday
from the tiny icy panes
beyond which, invisibly, the defenestration
                    of the apostles goes on.

ORIGINS

LAWRENCE MILLMAN

THE ORIGIN OF EDITORS

Odysseus was a pretty stupid guy. If you took away his body, you'd be taking away everything, because his brain was completely at the service of his massive strength. This fact rankled him. He knew that if he were forced to confront Penelope's suitors in a battle of wits, he'd lose by a very wide margin. Therefore, to acquire in knowledge what he already possessed in brawn, Odysseus began studying the texts of the Ancients: he poured over Proust, Joyce, Wodehouse, Updike, and Robert Service. Sure enough, these authors caused him to think for the first time. It was beautiful. When he described the sensation to Penelope, she looked quite proud: "Oh darling. I knew you could do it." Soon Odysseus became adept in the subtle art of making discriminations; for example, he tossed aside Updike and Robert Service in favor of more pithy texts. And not long after that, he was ready to attempt a text of his own; he decided to compose an exegesis of his own travels, omitting nothing. While he was thus engaged, the suitors were slyly sneaking into Penelope's chamber and having their way with her. Odysseus himself now only rarely visited his wife's chamber and then only for a critical commentary on his text, which was nearing completion. On one of these rare visits, however, he surprised a suitor there. The suitor immediately grabbed his sword; Odysseus took up his own weapon, which—

owing to a general flabbiness in his arms—he now found impossible to wield. Needless to say, he was no match for the suitor, who promptly ran him through twice. The victorious suitor then began to read the text. On his face was a look of distinct interest. He remarked to Penelope: "Your man may have been stupid, but his stuff shows promise. Let me take this home for a few nights and play around with it. I think I can turn it into something very fine indeed." True to his word, the suitor reworked Odysseus' manuscript until it was publishable. Before long, it was brought out in a special posthumous edition, to celebrate which Penelope and the suitor got married.

THE ORIGIN OF INSURANCE AGENTS

A young boy was wadding up pieces of paper. His parents bought him only reams of the very best paper, then he'd proceed to write "I am a bird" on each piece before wadding it up and throwing it away. "And at such an early age," his parents remarked.

On a fine spring day, one of his wadded papers took wing. It flew right out the window and alighted in a nearby tree and began to sing jubilantly, no doubt celebrating its freedom. It sang all through the summer and into the autumn. Then it died. It couldn't tolerate the cold weather.

The boy was disconsolate. His parents tried to cheer him up with toy soldiers and a baseball bat and a football, but each new gift brought on a fresh flow of tears. The boy said he only wanted to hear singing in the trees. "But it's winter," his parents told him. "But it wasn't a real bird," he replied. In desperation, his parents bought him a parakeet in a cage. Despite the fact that it was winter, the bird sang. It was cute and it sang. The boy was still not pleased. He grabbed the bird and wadded it up and threw it out the window. It fell soundlessly to the ground. "Now there's a real bird for you," he said.

The boy never trusted paper again. When he grew up, he became an insurance agent.

THE ORIGIN OF TELEPHONES

Being a decentralized creature, the brontosaurus had a hard time monitoring its various body parts. Often the head would go in one direction, the tail in another, and the legs would trek off in still a third direction. The poor beast would not only arrive at the wrong destination, but it would arrive there with a lot of pulled muscles and strained ligaments to boot. At long last, a particularly enterprising brontosaurus decided that enough was enough: if the species were to survive, it needed revamping. So this smart fellow installed six primitive speaking boxes in strategic parts of his own body, placing them in the head, the front legs, the hind legs, and the ass. In this way, communication was established between his own remote outposts. Now any body section could notify any other body section of a decision to move; and the movement could be synchronized after the decision was put to a vote. This brontosaurus did, in fact, last an entire year without going in the opposite direction of himself. As time passed, his invention was modernized. Today we no longer need speaking boxes in so many different places. Only one is necessary: the one in the ass.

THE ORIGIN OF ALCOHOLISM

Though childless himself, my friend Clint had a way with kids. He'd jump right into the sandbox with them and spend long hours helping them build their little sandcastles. All this sand would give Clint a powerful thirst and he'd usually end the day with a few beers at the local bar. Soon he was spending his afternoons as well as his evenings at the bar. And then he abandoned playing with kids altogether. He was now a confirmed heavy drinker. He'd sit in a corner muttering grim things about the end of the world, interrupting himself only to order another whiskey sour. "All our castles are made of sand, and they'll topple, oh how they'll topple, before long," he'd tell anyone who'd listen. The other customers regarded him with a mixture of pity and annoyance. They stopped bringing their wives to the bar for fear of Clint's frightening them with his apocalyptic talk. But he just babbled on, and it became virtually impossible to get him home when the bar closed. At last, he was removed to a local alcoholic's home for a dry-out. There he was interviewed by a guidance counselor who asked him what he wanted to do with his life. "Nothing," he said not without emotion. He was then handed over to a psychiatrist who told him that his attitude was rather bleak, wasn't it? Clint nodded in the affirmative. The psychiatrist told him that he only needed to watch little children at their games, observe the joy and exuberance with which they related to each other, to know that the world wasn't coming to an end. When Clint was released, he did begin to observe children. He watched them in their sandboxes with their little shovels and pails. Finally, he could no longer resist it and he joined them. He taught them all he knew about building sand castles in shapes they never dreamed of. But all that sand made him very thirsty.

THE ORIGIN OF PRIVATE PROPERTY

One afternoon I came back from school to discover that a train had crashed into our house. The downstairs was a mess and the upstairs had disappeared completely, being now a part of the downstairs. My father was furious. "Get rid of these fuckin' corpses," he yelled, "else there won't be any movies this week." My brother and I dutifully buried the bodies of the passengers in the backyard, next to Rover. When we came back in, father was still fuming. "How in hell are we going to get that train out of here?" My brother and I exchanged uneager glances. I tried pushing and only got a youthful hernia for my efforts. My brother found a dolly, but couldn't manage to raise the train onto it. Father himself kicked the engine so hard that he broke his kneecap and three toes. And mother couldn't even reach the kitchen to make us all a cup of tea. A few of the neighbors tried to help, but at last we resigned ourselves to living with the train. After a while, we got used to it. We ate in the dining car and slept in the Pullman. Though the house itself had begun to deteriorate, the train, made of stronger stuff, remained. And soon we only had the train to call our own. The town council, however, decided that it was an eyesore and notified us that they were going to dispose of it. Father objected. "This train is our home," he said. "How can you talk about disposing of our home?" His protests fell on deaf ears. We woke up one winter morning and our home was moving. A fleet of thirty tow-trucks yoked together like oxen was hauling us away. Suddenly, one of the trucks slipped on the icy road and the rest of them slipped as well and our train ploughed right into a house. The family was just finishing a breakfast which proved to be their last. We jumped out and took immediate possession. Father found some hunting rifles in the broom closet and told my brother and me to stand guard at the windows. "Now, if anyone disputes our right to this house, he'll get his balls blown from here to Baton Rouge," he said. But years passed, and still no one seemed interested in claiming the house, which father always assumed was because the previous owners left no heirs. Myself, I think that people might have been a little put off by the train, which we could never get rid of.

THE ORIGIN OF RELIGION

The Buddha was so wealthy, he could afford to experiment with chauffeurs. He never had the same chauffeur for more than one day. Sometimes it was even less than that. He might be driven to the corner drugstore simply for a laxative, and a new chauffeur would have to be found to drive him home; once home, he might dispose of the new chauffeur immediately. The abandoned chauffeurs came to resent this treatment. They began to gather in empty warehouses to voice their complaints. At one of these meetings, an especially vocal ex-chauffeur of the Buddha's announced: "We must be treated in the manner to which we would like to be accustomed, or ELSE. In short, we must unionize." But by the time the chauffeurs were able to unionize, the Buddha had begun to experiment around with different selves, replacing an old self with a new one each day if not sooner. Arriving at his mansion with a list of their demands, the chauffeurs found that the Buddha had already changed into Roy Rogers and God knows, even a good union member must submit to the King of the Cowboys. The chauffeurs bowed low and apologized for their intrusion. In time, they learned to be more satisfied with their lot. They even started to attend old Roy Rogers movies.

SIX POEMS

JUSTO JORGE PADRÓN

Translated from the Spanish by Louis M. Bourne

TRANSLATOR'S NOTE. *Justo Jorge Padrón belongs to a young group of Spanish poets whose first wave was the so-called "Venetians," dating from Pere Gimferrer's Arde el mar ("The Sea Blazes," 1966) with its legacy of Rubén Darío's Modernism. They are noted for a greater concentration on the autonomy of language and fantasy (a prolongation of Surrealism) than one finds in the two previous generations of post-Spanish Civil War poets. Like his contemporary, Antonio Colinas, Padrón relishes his nostalgic and neo-Romantic moments, but whereas Colinas waxes sensuous and languid, Padrón, more varied and fitful, ranges from tender love to a damned passion, to the beauty and terror of his occasionally frenetic imagination. Yet in a poetry of moods, he is capable of facing the blackest reality of atomic destruction or the fresh innocence of a newborn earth. His poems frequently take place at night, in the controlled compulsion of his visions.*

Born in the city of Las Palmas, Grand Canary Island, on October 1, 1943, Justo Jorge Padrón received his high school education in his native city and studied law, philosophy, and liberal arts at Barcelona University. He extended his studies in Paris and Stockholm. For seven years he maintained a legal practice, until he gave it up to devote himself entirely to literature. Apart from lecturing at universities and cultural centers in Asia, Europe, and Latin America, Padrón has written scripts for Spanish film, radio, and television. He currently lives in Madrid.

His poetic works consist of the following titles: Los oscuros fuegos *("The Dark Fires," 1971; Second Prize in the Adonais Awards of 1970),* Mar de la noche *("Sea of the Night," 1973; Boscán Award, 1972),* Los círculos del Infierno *("The Circles of Hell," 1976; Fasten-*

rath Award of the Spanish Royal Academy of the Language, 1972–77, for the best book of poems published between 1972 and 1976, and the Biennial Award of the Swedish Writers Association, 1976–77), Ningún ruido, ningún silencio. Antología poética 1971–1976 *("No Noise, No Silence: Selected Poems 1971–1976," 1978),* El abedul en llamas *("The Birch Tree in Flames," 1978),* Otesnita *("Otesnita," 1979), and* Obra poética 1971–1980 *("Poetic Works: 1971–1980," 1980) which includes twenty poems from a forthcoming book.*

Along with his poetic creation, Padrón also translates poetry and writes essays. His role as introducer of the poetry of northern Europe to the Spanish-speaking world has been such that Swedish Academy Member Artur Lundkvist regards him as "the essential mediator between Nordic and Spanish literatures." His contributions to the fields of criticism and translation include: La nueva poesía sueca *("The New Swedish Poetry," 1972; International Award of the Swedish Academy of the Language, 1972, and International Award of the Lundkvist Foundation, 1972),* La poesía contemporánea noruega *("Contemporary Norwegian Poetry," 1973; International Award of the National Institute of Norwegian Culture, 1973),* El modernismo en la poesía sueca *("Modernism in Swedish Poetry," 1973),* Panorama de la narrativa Islandesa contemporánea *("Panorama of the Contemporary Icelandic Narrative," 1974),* Paradisets Skugga *(1974, selected poems of Vicente Aleixandre, translated into Swedish in collaboration with Artur Lundkvist),* La poesía nórdica de la posguerra *("Postwar Nordic Poetry," 1974, essays on Swedish, Norwegian, Danish, Finnish, and Icelandic poetry),* Antología de Maria Wine *("Selected Poems of Maria Wine," 1977), and* La poesía española desde la Posguerra *("Postwar Spanish Poetry," 1980, panoramic essays on European poets and poetry, 1950–80).*

For Padrón, the poem arises when a "fraction of time becomes paralyzed and our consciousness sees and hears the world in its essential truth." Despite his close attention to the music and metrics of Spanish, Padrón strives, as few of his generation, to balance with his own cosmogonic perspective a concern for language with the claims of emotion, concept, and imagination. Defining poetry as "the most intense life directed toward the ultimate knowledge of the Cosmos," he emphasizes intuition and revelation as a means of grasping "the universal mystery." The risky, if stark, adventure of his feelings and apperceptions takes precedence over reactions to his historical context.

LIKE SOMEONE SPRINGING UP FROM AUTUMN

For Julio and Leandro Silva

"Are you here?"
"We're all dead," I replied gloomily.
And without paying us the least attention,
He came in like one more member
Of the house.
He arrived like someone springing up from autumn,
From a sorrow,
Maybe even further away, from a forgotten dream.
And he unloaded his bundle of joy
In the grim corners.
He smoothed down his weary hair
Of rain and winds.
He sat down beside us
And lived all the aromas
Of the room. He gave us
His simple heart,
Lit up the songs, now lost,
From water and fires.
He urged us to go on,
Not to suffer that bitter death,
And he spread out before us
The roads that lead to life.
He embraced us in the end one by one,
And a powerful light suffused our lips.
With watery eyes,
We accompanied him to the horizon.
We asked him for a last word:
"What name can we remember you by?"
The voice, almost smoke,
Scarcely reached us.
And since then our lives
Have been only waiting, waiting for a stranger.

ANOTHER BURNING DISTANCE

For Anne and Edmond Vandercammer

To raise a blank sheet of paper and see the poem,
As if my gaze could probe
Another burning distance where it was written
By the hand of a chance that precedes me.
To cross through the dense forest of sight
With a keen and dogged gleam.
And so, with the calm of controlled fire,
To keep it in its future truth,
I start to retrieve the mysterious lines
Of that other presence slipping away
In the blinding light of its origin.

THE TAMER

Homage to Octavio Paz

The tamer took his place in the ring,
In the midst of the silence and people,
Before the chasm of life
And the judgment of men.
He came from the sun and brought a mirror
Of wild transparencies
And a secret legacy of intelligence and light.
His face lined with grave strength
Projected the proud eyes of a stern
Forsaken breed,
To which he, perhaps better than anyone,
Gave clarity and vigor, feeling and a way.
Many, every day more,
Came from different latitudes and races
With the sole aim of learning his command.

Suddenly the tamer revealed some frenzied birds
That opened up a bright and hidden vertigo,
And from his hands sprang wild beasts with sluggish movements
Exploding with a flash of beauty in the mind.
Butterflies of sun as gentle as smiles
Or fish probing with blades of fright.
Strange animals crossing from mystery
To silence, discovering its imprisoned blood.
And those others that stirred up dreams
And visions that few could hope to glimpse.
All the animals of language
Sporting their splendor,
Becoming horizons, flames, flight and existence,
Loveliness unleashed, and power,
Before the blue gaze of their master.

GAZELLE OF WATER

You arrived limpid as a gazelle of water
That would suddenly spring up
In the night forest of my body
And turn my bleak prison
Into a blazing lamp.

I have lived
The gadflies of hate and disgrace,
Blameworthy negligence,
My defenseless promises and their dreams.
I have seen cathedrals of shadow rise up,
Of vanity or lies, and preserved
The insatiable hope of waiting for you.

Let us live this never-repeated urge,
Knowing that after our fire
Only fear and ashes will remain,
The desolation, the rain, and the forgetting.

Hug me, for only your embrace
Gives me the image of the earth, the water,
Conquered space, the word and the music,
The warm radiance of grasses,
You, unique, blue planet, world my own.

LONELINESS AMONG THE SANDS

The seagull glides down and halts
In the crystal of the air
Like a tear searching for a face.

The night breeze
Draws near with stars. The sea unfolds
A wordless sobbing that death has taught it.

Trees bowed and
Bitten by the thirstiest light and salt.

Loneliness among the sands. The cold
Of the first shadows grows.

Only her absence
Burns in the dark earth.

THE SUICIDE

The injection of death dissolves
With the last hope.
Now from far away the birds and poplars come.
All the faces converge, the gentle geography.
The dark rivers of his body shudder;
He hears a slow and soundless voyage of needles,

A frozen bubble, a mirror and its shadow.
They advance, now he cannot halt
The fever of their footsteps, their rising growth,
Nor put to sleep the wounds they leave behind.
As he feels how the fire in his forest leaps up.
How the smoke climbs up around his eyes,
And veins, blood vessels, and blood burst with such a din.
What a strange sleeping wind wakes up
And a huge head sprouts from his chest.
His teeth are icy whirlwinds.
They are storms of vertical stones
Now aiming at the heart.

FOUR POEMS

ANTONIO CISNEROS

Translated from the Spanish by Maureen Ahearn, William Rowe, and David Tipton

WINTER AGAIN + "DOS INDIOS" BY ALFREDO BRYCE

> *—I'm returning to Peru, he said, smiling and optimistic. But neither the smile nor the optimism suited him—*

A trough of low pressure has arrived with the winds from the
    north—precipitation
1.4 inches and humidity 90%. And I go on living in Europe.
I shall have to leave with the tide/find out how much it is
    to Lima.
For I've no umbrella,
I've never had an umbrella,
no one in Lima has an umbrella.
True I've bought 2 or 3 since I've been living at the bottom
    of the sea,
but I've lost them just as I've been losing my friends and my
    wives/wasting my time.
Somehow or other I'm going to put a roof over my head—
                              The Times,
    Le monde, or *Nice Matin*—
and bury myself among the winds and waves, leaving my shack:
    the time has come.

To leave my shack, for if I don't
I'll have to buy a double bed
   a pair of rubber boots
   and a gas heater,
and then I'll never know the price of a ticket to Peru.
I'll remain among the villas, flitting among the tribes of Nice
  who'll go on telling me
the same things as a family photo of an old family that I've
  never met.

I've got to fly to Lima, though I'm afraid
I'll not be able to recognize myself in the photo/in my own
  family photograph.
     [DT]

ON THE CLICHE

It's not my fault if it's raining and my own skin is the wall
  that encloses the besieged city
     cold, darkness
and fast cars their headlamps shining through the water like
  cat's eyes,
   like the Flanders legions:
provisions, canons, catapults arm an encampment in cattle fields
  and hills,
    the state of siege
is an image of courtly love and in the paintings of the mad
  an image of the soul,
    and the eyes of a cat
always shine when the air's black and everyone knows it and at
  night no one could confuse them with dogs or girls escaping
  from their houses,
     between rain
and the liver ice and darkness will fit if you're not talking
  about the Tropics,
    as for the besieged city

there's nothing more to say, on both sides of the high walls
    they bury their dead without the least ceremony,
                              under the water
drums beat prudently, the soldiers piss in the grass and down
    wind, no one bothers with fire arrows or the cauldron of
    boiling water,
                    death, old age
and in general the things that have to do with the end are repre-
    sented by quiet drums, flutterings of the owl that brings calm,
    a pause and silence
to bury the dead, here the symbol says that our good side helps
    or eliminates the bad,
                      and so salvation
is this sun that spins among the roofs like a Turner painting,
    it's not my fault, nordic and watery,
                      the winter lights
high, strange, oblique, appreciated, always come suddenly
    and nearly always on time,
                    with death
images come to an end but it's right to point out that in those
    lights there's no door or ladder climbing to Paradise
                      popular image
of Saul, Elias, Jacob, Assumption of the Virgin, Ascension of
    Christ,
                    it's the orange tree
that grows fat in the land of the men who are dead, symbol of
    Materialism, and they put their foot in it where they can't
    get it out again:
there's no symbol or name for this.
                [WR]

YOUR HEAD LIKE AN ITALIAN ARCHANGEL'S

I (*Jutka*)
Your Italian archangel's head doesn't fit those eyes that came
    on horseback from beyond the Urals.

But you're as beautiful as a fruit out of season.
(And you tell me that your mother's face is the same as that
    of ancient Hun women.)
You love strong wine in abundance—*el mar de España,* you say
    —and curse
the light of a sentry at midnight. And you don't have any
    papers.

II *(to Jutka from her father)*
—"The labyrinth, Jutka, the labyrinth. Not a bit of the rebel.
    You know nothing
about the violin (which you detest) nor of hunger.
You were born and our house was a house overcome by war. Yet
    that winter
we still had peppers and salted pork (and nights of silence).
You know nothing of the time when glory was a red rat—my
    poppy—roasted in the trenches.
Your labyrinth, Jutka, your labyrinth. Of lunatics, not rebels.
The tall grasses grow in perfect silence. And you fear so much
    peace.
I love peace (not the peace of the lamb). And I the child of
    the plague, I rebel.
And don't look that way. Here no one's sold his soul to the
    devil, nor am I bad seed.
Mercury shines upon the fresh earth.
Kiss my hands, Jutka. Go to bed."

III
Behind that door—right now—men and rats are gnawing at your
    father's old memory
awaiting the laurel dream.
*The young warriors have reached the street of the Fish. Uncle
    Miska—already dead this Lent—shouts out in bad Russian:
    to hell with war, gentleman, the war is over.*
And you dream too. But your dreams are not about soldiers in the
    street of the Fish.
(Silence of the canon and the rat—red as a poppy.)

IV

You were born when the moss was growing old between the new
    bridges over the river.
Order and construction of socialism.
And the memory of war was just a fleck of ash on the winter wind.
Mild days in the sun on the green hills.
But order was also a lament or a muffled cry beneath the
    searchlights
and the peace of the lamb
—the smile of someone looking for a cottage in the sun on
    the green hills.

                  (You kiss his hands.)

V *(Jutka's dream)*
The White Guard: Denikin
in the fields of the Ukraine.
The Red Guard rides the frontier.
It accepts neither the armistice nor respite.
(Death to Denikin
and death to the Polish bandits).
The wild ducks honk above a wood of firs.

VI

The ducks honk and the young make love beneath a sky
    blue as their jeans.
They know nothing of the violin nor light opera in the great
    labyrinth. They know nothing
about the time of the rats. And they fear the silence at
    midnight.
The big black cars that cross the Danube (blue) are testimony
to some old men—rebels and well ordered like straight hair.

                          [MA & DT]

CONTEMPLATING THE MEDITERRANEAN +
LEONARD COHEN

The first thing you do is throw stones at seagulls, though you
    know you'll never touch them in flight or on the ground.
Then the literary part.
And gradually you sink into that big postcard you'd never dare
    send anyone.
Blue sea/white seagulls/blue sky—paler than the sea/round sun/
    warm waters—to the eye at any rate/pine trees/geraniums/
    cliffs/rocks.
In the background a ship of the Italian Line.
You think about bridges and constellations and sextants and that
    booze-up with good Chianti the day Bernales left for Rome.
It was a wharf in Callao and yet the remains of Argonauts which
    reached that port were the same ones that wash up on this
    beach,
as if you always had to live on the side where the horizon ends.
And the seaweed gets tangled round the corpses not just of famous
    victims but of neighbors you've forgotten and suddenly
    remember
        Suzanne takes you down
        to her place near the river
And you end up sending postcards to the dead of two generations.
And among your dead you insert the man who's standing on the
    highest rock on the beach
        you can hear the boats go by
to keep an eye on that wind, supervise the movement of the waters,
    wave a flag at you when the ship returns to the anchorage it
    left from.
        you can stay the night beside her
And one fine day under a high/blue/clear sky—it'll go down in
    the annals of Lima—the remains of that ship without remorse
    now or anything left to save, will come to anchor in the sand.
        and you know that she's half crazy
like the lungless walrus thrown up by the waters in midsummer,
    you won't find the beginning or end of it—nor its place in
    history.
        but that's why you want to be there

You only know that the salt waters have delivered it from violent
   decomposition, from the plague, if you consider its size,
   species, condition.
And when you get to the beach you'll become sand among the sand,
   so fast even the quickest flies won't manage to bite you.
   and she feeds you tea and oranges
   that come all the way from China
Let's agree that you've died under the harpoons of foreign
   ships, under viruses of other oceans and dominions.
   Suzanne takes your hand
   and she leads you to the river
   she is wearing rags and feathers
   from Salvation Army counters
And now you see things more clearly than the back of a sole
   in the net, than a cock cleaned in boiling water.
You're no longer a slavering skeleton, an island without
   history:
you're the sand that builds up at the door of your house,
   once and for all.

                    [WR]

STRAY DOGS

GEOFFREY RIPS

I think she wore a brown dress. Walking toward me on the street. I think it was a brown dress. No. I think she was three and wore a ballet costume.

Parker doesn't like ideas. He says, "Let's go bowling." He rolls the ball four times down the lane. The first time the pin farthest back on the right side goes down. The second time the front pin and five behind it fall. The pins on the left stand in a triangle. It is exact. The third time the pin farthest back on the right side falls down. The fourth time he lets the ball go at the top of the lane, turns away, and begins walking toward the exit. He walks out the door without looking back.

Now I think it may have been blue and brown hair hanging past her shoulders.

Parker took me to meet Bruno in his art gallery. "It was, sadly enough, the perfect design," Bruno says. "I cannot hang a painting, I cannot introduce a ball, a box, a piece of wood, or everything is lost. Look . . ." The shadows of one wall cut the shadows of another. The floor ran to the white walls that swept into the shadows. The sky was blue through the windows. I had no desire to leave. Even a second's glance at a shadow brought a feeling of great calm. I followed a wall until it led me into a corner. And there I stopped. After a few minutes I began to notice the faint smell of dog's breath.

Parker says, "Later we should try this bowling one more time. I have some theories to kill."

She is coming toward me. I thought she was younger, her hair less blonde. No.

We watch the ferry leave for Staten Island. The log pilings moan and creak. If I see her again, I'll remember. I think she wore red. The wind lifted the ends of her hair.

The cracks in the sidewalk are stained a urine color. Nestor is telling the story of the Yorkshire terrier. "This morning I stepped on a Yorkshire terrier. Its legs went out to the sides. It felt like a rubber dog."

Four boys holding cans chase a rat out of an alley. The rat runs along the front of a building and up to the front door, where it stops. One of the boys pours a soft drink on the rat's head. It shakes its head and runs out from the doorway toward the street. A second boy hits the rat with a soft-drink can. The rat flips over on its back and then flips again to its feet. It runs into the street. The boys run after it.

"Just like the dog," Nestor says. "It popped up on all fours and ran off. Hard to fathom the lower animals."

"Last night I had a dream," I said. "Nestor was trying to lay Cleo. They ran around and around the house. I was lying on the living room floor listening to their progress through the various rooms. Each time they stepped over me, my prick got hard."

We come to a store selling fish. Carp float in tanks at the window. Some slowly wave their fins. Some float upside down, their mouths at the surface of the water. Parker buys a pound of mussels. He holds the dripping, waxy white paper away from his body. We walk to Parker's place.

"Last night I met a wrench musician," Parker tells us. "He said he began with jars of water. Then he moved on to saws. I heard him play the saw. He plays for Chattaqua—upstate, in Ohio, in Maine. In Clarion, Ohio, a mechanic told him he plays tunes by dropping his wrenches on a cement floor. The musician went to the mechanic's shop. They began by throwing wrenches in the air to hear the tones they made when they hit the floor. The musician recorded each tone in his notebook. Then they worked on a method of playing. They threw the wrenches in the air and struck them with a hammer as they fell. They found a wooden mallet that produced the clearest tone. Eventually, the mechanic devised a frame to hold the wrenches for striking with the mallet. Inside the frame, they are suspended on taut springs. The musician found a way to play the holes at the base of the wrench handles with a thin screwdriver. He bought the mechanic a new set of wrenches and returned to the Chattaqua circuit as a wrench musician."

We are now eating mussels with Parker. Cleo pours the wine. She asks, "If all the blondes in the city were murdered, do you think the brunettes would care?"

"Not unless they had once dyed their hair," Nestor says. "It's the only way to be moved by such madness."

Later Cleo goes into the back room. Her hair is red. I leave and walk by the river. The moon is already over New Jersey. Much farther west, birds still twitter in the twilight.

She is coming toward me now, her lips slightly parted. I thought her hair was blonde. She is waving. How can she walk? Her knees almost collide.

She asks, "What are you doing here?" She looks so familiar. She asks, "What do you think about my question? You didn't answer last night. If blondes were murdered, would the brunettes care?"

It's Cleo. I knew she looked familiar.

"It's all hypothetical, of course, but what do you think?"

I think about my dream. I say, "Let's have a drink and talk this over."

We walk. Who am I looking for?

"Another question," she says in the bar. "This time in the form of a statement: The destruction is so huge it cannot be reassembled. What do you think?"

"I give up," I say. I have the feeling we are in a bar cast adrift. We are passing monuments to our lives: New Jersey, the blinking traffic light outside the window.

"Okay," she says and starts to leave, tucking the ends of her pants into the tops of her boots. They are Duccio blue.

"I'm sorry," I say. "No answers." The spurs on my boots scrape the floor tiles.

I send her a copy of *The Green House*. I send her a copy of

Hopscotch. She sends a note back: "Our lives are like bad South American literature, even lower than the imitative North American kind. Stop. I love you. Stop."

If I can remember how she looks. Red hair. She steps over my prick.

I ask Nestor, "What color are her eyes?"

He says, "How do I know, man? I can tell you how many she's got if she'll stand still to let me count them."

I go to the gallery. Bruno is pacing. "I cannot stand still. Any place I sit down or even stand I know it is wrong. She has clear blue eyes, knees that almost touch, thighs like dark brown eggs, and a waist that is pure liquid. Her breasts, if I may say this, have the uneven weight that all men try desperately to balance. If I may go further, it is the immaculate imperfection for which art itself was created."

I do not ask Parker. I find him bowling. This time he is jerking the ball back as he turns it loose. "I am trying to create enough backspin to return the ball to me as soon as it touches a pin. The pin mustn't fall down. I almost got it the last time. I felt it start to roll back."

Parker stands in his socks at the top of the lane. He releases a ball. It rolls toward the pins, touches the first pin, and stops. The pin rocks back and forth and falls. Parker walks down the lane to retrieve the ball. "I just use the thumbhole. I think that's the key. Cleo tells me you wouldn't answer her questions the other day when you met. Particularly the one in the form of a statement. That upsets her, you know. She says you didn't seem to recognize her either. Her hair is red."

I walk back home through the paper box district. Corrugated cardboard fills the streets.

"He drew the line of demarcation with an easy hand. 'So much for Portugal. So much for Spain,' the Pope said. 'I once studied in my cell the work of Micheli da Calabria. Also that of Bellini. He was precise. It is a little-known fact, but I have always thought of myself as an artist.' He put the map aside and straightened his cassock."

Parker stops reading. "So much history in the hands of an artist. It is a shame."

Cleo says, "At least they didn't put gondolas on the Amazon or on the Plata either." She looks to Lisette, who is smiling at a postcard of Simone Martini's *Annunciation* taped to the wall.

One woman looking at another. Parker must think they are lesbians. I say, "It is interesting to watch the windows across the street. In one there is a woman in a purple dress smoking a cigarette. In another a woman in a green dress is also smoking. And down below there is another woman in a purple dress, but she is not smoking. That building is almost casual in its disregard for symmetry."

Cleo's hair is red. She walks behind me and whispers, "If Parker starts talking about bowling, take me to get coffee."

Parker sits facing Lisette. "It is another simple case of mis-direction. A Pope divides the world. And they let bowlers, teams in striped shirts drinking beer, they let them fiddle with the im-maculate geometry of a bowling lane—the long horizontal, the rotating sphere, the imaginary triangle at the mercy of fools."

Cleo walks to the door and waves to Parker. She grabs me by the sleeve and pulls me after her.

We sit at a counter drinking coffee. "I can't help thinking," she says, "that I dream about you every night. You don't look the same as you do now, of course. You don't even look the same from one night to the next. But it is you."

I continue sipping coffee. Her hand moves up and down my thigh.

"Don't worry about Parker," Cleo tells me. "He's too caught up with bowling. Last night we spent two hours with his thumb and index finger on my shoulder trying to measure the slightest changes of pressure against my skin. He asked me to tell him each time I felt the pressure lessen or felt it grow. Some nights I don't mind pleasing him this way."

We follow the long sidewalk that runs by the park. The cracks in the sidewalk run west and east. The twigs and branches that lie on the sidewalk also lie in that direction.

I ask, "Wasn't your hair slightly more blonde? Don't you wear a red dress?"

"No," she says. Her dress is tan.

We stop by a bench and sit down. "Today I found a postcard,"

I say. "It is a photograph of a drawing by Keats of a Grecian urn. Should I show you the card or should I describe it?"

"Do both," she says.

I hand her the card and begin. "Swans looking like ducks form the handles of the urn. A woman carries a spear. The arm of a naked warrior rises from the surface of the vase. There is a garland. There are uneven patterns, one made of arches. There are no pipes. Things are not quite still."

"Thank you," Cleo says. "I wouldn't have known otherwise."

We walk farther. Her hair is red.

We agree to meet in a lobby. "The next time Parker mentions bowling," she says, "even if you're not there. Even though this has nothing to do with Parker."

Cleo kisses my cheek. She leaves. Her dress is tan. Her hips. Her shoes strike sound from the sidewalk, then the pavement, then marble steps, and later a wooden floor as she enters a building.

I find Bruno sitting on the curb in front of the gallery. "It is closed," he says, "for now or for good, I don't know. I felt like a pinball, like something misplaced. All day I have been sitting here with a rock trying to throw it through one of the windows. But I cannot tell which one. Not this one and not that one either. I am no match for so much perfection."

She is coming toward me now. Her hair is red. We meet beside a pillar in the lobby. We embrace. Her waist presses my waist. We walk to my room. Her knees almost collide. As I open the door to my room, a draft lifts the ends of her hair.

We walk by the river. Cleo puts her arm around my waist. We walk out on an abandoned pier. A small boy chases a hoop around us. It falls through a gap in the boardwalk. The boy looks down through the slats at the water. The smokestacks of the factories across the river are almost pink. Cleo says, "Maybe I was wrong. Maybe you weren't the one in my dreams."

I walk with her to the bowling alley to find Parker. Cleo holds my hand. We walk to the door of the bowling alley. But I see her coming toward me now. Her dress is red. No. She is wearing a brown dress. The wind lifts the ends of her hair.

FIVE POEMS

MARIO CESARINY

*Translated from the Portuguese by Jean R. Longland
and Jonathan Griffen*

SPIRITUAL EXERCISE

It is necessary to say rose instead of idea
it is necessary to say blue instead of panther
it is necessary to say fever instead of innocence
it is necessary to say the world instead of a man

It is necessary to say candelabrum instead of arcanum
it is necessary to say For Ever instead of Now
it is necessary to say The Day instead of A Year
it is necessary to say Mary instead of dawn

                                                    [JRL]

I IN 1951

*"The seagulls and taménidas live in harmony . . . The seagulls are
white and the taménidas let out horrible screams . . . "—Carlos
Wallenstein,* A Carta e o Mundo

I in 1951 picking up (discreetly) a cigarette end (usable)
in a downtown café through being incapable alas for them

of writing my verses without really fulfilling
in them and around them my own unity
—smoking, that is.

This unity, which is not brilliant, is what nobody expected
to see in a book with verses. But it's the truth. It denotes
my essential lack of hygiene (not of tobacco)
and a noteworthy absence (not of money) of scruples.

Armando, who is writing across from me
his very own poem, is smoking too.

We smoke like desperate men we write desperately
and no position in the world (it seems to me) is higher
more frightening and violent incompatible and comforting
than this one of getting other people's tobacco free
(except things like shame, naturally,
and shrouds)

(As far as is known) this is the first time
a poet has written so low (at the level of other people's butts)
Here, and nowhere else, scintillates that thing conditionalism
that has been talked of so long and is discreetly
placed (like the one who picks them up.)

Let it all serve as a lesson for people present and future
in the (various) taménidas of local poetry
—Rather to go around relatively fed up
rather with tobacco than with Cesariny
(Mário) de Vasconcelos

                    [JRL]

VOICE ON THE HILLS OF ALMADA

"Hello sun! Hello ten-minute dog!
Good morning up there in the sky, far away from the earth!
You ought to come inside there with us,
shine inside there, beautiful as fire on the sea!
You would learn to turn pale you would learn to throw up
when the smoke is too much and it tortures. You
would throw up . . . rays!

"But you can't, we know
you can't, we know
you are bound by a contract
up there in the sky like us down here on the earth.
Oh sun, good sun, it's funny! They've caught you.
They've put a collar on you, hey sun, you're bound!
You're forbidden to go down there, hear?
You're forbidden to go down along there with us.
Hey sun, what do you say? All forbidden.
On your right side, on your left side,
in front and in back, over and under, well! anyway at all
it's forbidden. It's funny. It's horrible. It's the way things are.
And so—goodbye! Until we see you again some day!
Until we see you again, hey you scared dog, coming with us
for ten minutes every morning!"

Ten minutes it takes from home to the factory
Ten minutes of sun at eight in the morning
Ten minutes of light, ten measured minutes

But in spite of the thick filthy smoke
these men adore the caress of a sun
that shines for twelve hours and cuddles the people of the world
And more: they speak softly
of an endless dawn of an unfoolhardy light
that at eight in the morning gives a virile salute
the ten-minute sun of the working classes

[JRL]

DISCOURSE TO PRINCE EPAMINONDAS,
A YOUTH WITH A GREAT FUTURE

Say goodbye to truths
the great ones before the small ones
your own sooner than any others
open up a pit and bury them
at your side
first the ones they imposed on you you were not a fighter yet
and had no blotch except an outlandish name
then the ones you put on painfully as you grow up
the truth of bread the truth of tears

since you are not a flower or a lute or a lullaby or a star
then those you win with your semen
where the morning raises an empty mirror
and a child is crying between clouds and abysses
then those they will place above your portrait
when you will have furnished them the great memory
they all expect so much because they expect it of you

Nothing then, only you and your silence
and coral veins tearing our wrists
At last, my lord, we shall be free to pass
over the naked plain
your body with clouds for shoulders
my hands full of white beards
There'll be no more stay nor shelter nor arrival
but a quadrature of fire above our heads
and a stone road as far as the end of lights
and a silence of death at our passing

                                    [JG]

JULIAN THE LOVERS

Now we have nothing to do on the face of the earth
    let us wait with closed eyes for the passing
    of the wind
said I   said I
for it's above the white eucharist of your breast that
    there rise the level palaces of water
in the dark   in the dark
someone will take us away touching with one finger
    us tremulous, stretched out, we shall die of
    having known each other so well
and then?   and then?
then the halo of some blue ribbon in the mallet left
    lying on the stone of a dream
but the grand rooms?   and the house?
and the dog which followed us?
your face my face
this tall man
                    the Sun
                    [JG]

FIVE POEMS

ANTÓNIO OSÓRIO

Translated from the Portuguese and introduced by
Giovanni Pontiero

THE LYRIC POETRY OF ANTÓNIO OSÓRIO

Giovanni Pontiero

> Learn to read between the lines,
> into a tense and fiery hand,
> into the rope or stone that destroys us,
> into this dazed love
> and bitter undulation
> of captive sea-horses.
>
> Then judge,
> ourselves as well, unsparingly.
>
> ("To Posterity")

António Osório was born in Setúbal, Portugal, in 1933, the son of a Portuguese father and Italian mother. A lawyer by profession, he resides in Lisbon.

While still in his early twenties, Osório became one of the guiding spirits of the literary journal *Anteu* (1954). His first book of poems *A Raiz Afectuosa* ("*The Tender Root*") appeared in 1972. Two years later, he published *A Mitologia Fadista* ("*The*

Mythology of Fate") one of many sociological essays to appear in various learned periodicals and concerned with the myths that influence everyday life in Portugal.

In 1978, Osório published a second book of poems, entitled *A Ignorância da Morte* (*"Ignorance of Death"*)—a book comprising two separate collections: *Aldeia de Irmãos* (*"Fraternal Village"*) and *A Matéria Volátil* (*"Volatile Matter"*).

Osório's poems have also appeared in a number of anthologies, notably *800 Anos de Poesia Portuguesa* (*"800 Years of Portuguese Poetry"*). In recent years, selections of his verse have been translated into French, Spanish, German, Rumanian, and now English.

In Brazil, a new anthology of Osório's poetry is currently being edited by the distinguished Southern Brazilian poet Carlos Nejar. This will be published shortly under the title *Emigrante do Paraíso* (*"Emigrant from Paradise"*).

Portuguese critics have hailed a new Romanticism in Osório's lyric verse with its salient qualities of simplicity and truth, purged of any intellectual pedantry. Serene and controlled, the poet recreates his own inner spirit and that of the universe by means of natural and spontaneous forms of expression. A master of clear, unforced statements and an instinctive refinement, his verses capture basic human experiences within a broad framework of verbal myths. Displaying a marked preference for short, intense lyrics, Osório illuminates humble manifestations of ordinary life with art and grace. Spontaneous sentiments establish fraternal bonds with those objects and people to whom he feels instinctively drawn.

The poet's origins and spiritual roots are evoked with profound respect. The sacred memory of his ancestors is nourished with all the conviction of an inherited religion: "Scribe and narrator of lives and processes, I have learned to absolve myself of childhood" (*"Ponte Vecchio"*).

Crystalline and fluent, these poems make an immediate impression with their purity of sound and meaning. A quiet trust governs the most fleeting observation.

Ancient and modern canons merge in this timeless lyricism and a reassuring humanity mitigates any doubts or regrets.

Yet, occasionally, Osório's deeply personal vision of the world can seem strange and pungent. The fragments of autobiography betray a painful awareness of dual forces in his cultural legacy—a contrast bordering upon conflict as he traces the threads of two great civilizations in his own spiritual make-up. An insistent perusal of the past expands into the pursuit of some lost paradise suspended between concrete reality and a metaphysical plane of intangible mysteries.

A principle of "ostinato rigore" (to quote Carlos Nejar) enables Osório to maintain his composure and reconcile warring allegiances. Precise images attest to the solemnity and riches of mortal existence, its potential and challenge espied in every gesture and expression of life.

"Ignorance of death" is conceived as a binding condition of survival—a fate shared by man, dog, cat, goat, and horse. For each category of existence responds to its own intransigent laws. A close study of the relationships between the species—human, animal, mineral, and botanical—suggests that man must ultimately be regarded as the most vulnerable creature of all, branded by a terrible pathos and absurdity, complicated by contradictory emotions and a fragile integrity—hence the relevance of Jorge Guillen's words that: "Las misérias del hombre/merecen compasión," a message reaffirmed by Osório as his own "tender root" penetrates the earth, digging deep until it reaches "the tiniest and most ancient vein of tears" ("The Tender Root").

THE ROAD PAVERS

They write in the road:
carefully
assembling
words.

They press them down
syllable by syllable,
selecting, uniting,
completing,
tapping them
gently into place
before moving on.

They sign their work
with mallet
and sweat.

THE DOGS

So many dogs. Disregarding
the shame
they lick our hands.

Their religion is mysterious.
Showing no fear
they gaze upon the countenance of their deity.

A privilege denied even to Moses.

ANTONIO

> I bambini sono teneri
> e feroci. Non sanno
> la differenza che c'è
> tra un corpo e la sua cenere.
>
> —*Eugenio Montale*

1
You like to stretch out on the ground.
One day you will learn the cost.

2
How is the firmament made?
or the inside of a tree?

3
How does one grow?
What is the soul like within?

4
Almost with the same eyes
(for yours cannot
be compared with mine)
we saw that animal appear.
An enormous rat, and no less inquisitive,
as it looks on in amusement.

5
How many days after death
does one return to life?

6
Initial residue
as one loses
one's first tooth.

Take note: by suffering
one grows old.

7
Daddy, does the world never end?

8
I never believed you capable
        of certain things
    —that you should kiss
that sloven,
unruffled mother
and then,

one by one,
her children,
six young pigs.

9
How does one reach heaven?
Do we simply close our eyes
and fly away?

10
The bliss
of playing alone
in your room.

If only verses could be written so.

11
What have we here?
An embalmed partridge.
Pretending to be alive?

12
I am a daddy, you say,
putting on a pair of large shoes.
You dream of what it means to be a man
and grow weary. Without heartache,
you then return to being a child.

HOUSE OF SEEDS

Sad not to possess a house of seeds.
Useless to love those idle particles,

or desire that they take root without hailstorm
and shoot up like a candle's flame.

Sad to pay a price for what must grow
that the lucerne should lose its sorrel hue upon penetrating the soil
and the Persian clover feed the mouths of the flock.

Sad that they should not refuse that dense, prodigal,
persistent enslavement, their vitality transfixed to the sun,
that they should not reckon their accounts like the peasant,
exacting the wages of machination from God and man.

MORTUARY ROOM

Smoke, some
flowers, inevitable
tears,
the awkward deposition,
the futile
disguise of sheets.

Hunger, sleep,
the rumble of condolences.
Enquiries
how it happened.
Trifling exchanges
about mortal things.

Anecdotes, smiles
and coffee.

The corpse is ready:
awaiting the stroke
of mercy.

WHAT IS IT, ZACH?

JAMES PURDY

Zach, a veteran of the Vietnam War, thirty years old, comes originally from Illinois. He is of an athletic build, and looks strong still despite his war injuries. Pete, eighteen, left his home in North Carolina after some trouble there, and has lived a hand-to-mouth existence since. Although thin and sensitive-looking, he also communicates a kind of vehement physical forcefulness, pronounced hurt, and deep anger.

PETE. I don't get any work of my own done now I'm telling you . . . All I do is cook for this veteran . . . I know I'm not a cook, but I had to tell him I was to get the job . . . No, he's not satisfied, or who knows . . . Anyhow I am learning to cook . . . I have to hang up now, I hear him coming.

(*Enter Zachary in his worn army uniform and high shoes.*)

ZACH. My phone bill was enough to break me this month . . . And you know I never use it . . . Don't you?

PETE. You call the druggist . . . When I could go for you just as well.

ZACH. That's one call a month, whereas . . .

PETE. You told me you wanted me to feel comfortable here the day you hired me . . . Well, using the phone is one way I can feel that . . . After all you won't let my friends call here . . .

ZACH. I think you have it easy here.

PETE (*goes to the stove and tastes the soup*). You do?

ZACH. You have very limited duties . . . What's that you're cooking tonight? (*Without waiting for an answer*) I'm half famished . . . Do you know something: I miss the army grub . . . Can you beat that? I miss that goddam awful chow!

PETE. Well, that's a nice compliment for my cooking! After I bend over the stove all day to please you.

ZACH. I didn't mean it that way, Pete. (*Sitting down*) I guess I'm like you in that one respect . . . You miss your friends and talk to them all the time on the telephone, but my buddies, my friends . . . are . . . beyond reach.

PETE (*interrupting*). If I can't cook better than some army mess sergeant you better fire me, Zach. (*Tastes some more of the food he is preparing*)

ZACH. Where is your chef's hat . . . I thought I told you always to wear a chef's hat . . . You remember what I found last night in the tomato sauce.

PETE. I sent the chef's hat to the laundry . . . Are you ready to eat now, Zach . . . Are you?

ZACH. Then why didn't you buy another chef's hat . . . Huh? I would have gladly given you the money . . . Why didn't you?

PETE. Are you ready for your first course, I say . . .

ZACH (*tying napkin around his neck*). All right . . . I'm ready . . . (*angry*) Sent his chef's hat to the laundry . . . I said I'm ready.

PETE (*tying his apron about his middle more tightly, and then slowly bringing in the soup*). (*Puts it down*) There! Now if that don't taste good . . .

ZACH (*queerly*). Don't ever be without a chef's hat again, you hear?

PETE. Try my soup . . .

ZACH. I want you always in a chef's hat. (*Begins to taste*) Something new, huh? (*Tastes audibly*) Mmm. Strange. Can't identify any of it . . .

PETE. I worked all day on that concoction.

ZACH. Here we go again on how hard you work to prepare one meal a day! It shouldn't take that long! You blame me for you not getting your work done when any ninny can make soup, and from scratch in half an hour . . .

PETE. And do the shopping, and the cleaning, and reading the recipe books.

ZACH. You told me you were a master chef when I hired you! Turns out you had trouble even boiling water!

PETE. Well what do you think of the soup, Zach?

ZACH. It's peculiar.

PETE. Peculiar?

ZACH. I told you I couldn't identify what's in it.

PETE. Well, for cripes sake, it has lots in it . . . That's what took so long. It has a whole head of cauliflower.

ZACH. Cauliflower is very expensive!

PETE. A few stalks of broccoli, celery, garlic, a carrot or so, potatoes to make it mashy, onions, and on account of we don't have a blender I have to chop all that fine, which takes a lot of pounding.

ZACH. Well there's something else here that escapes me. (*Tastes and looks sullen*) Do you clean the pot good after every use?

PETE. Of course I do . . . What do you think I am . . .

ZACH. You're immature for one thing, and for another you're a liar.

PETE. Let me taste that soup. (*He seizes the spoon from Zach, and tastes it.*) There ain't nothin' wrong with that soup, and you know it. It's not peculiar. It's good! It's too good for you.

ZACH. What?

PETE. You heard me . . . I should just open a can of store soup and you'd love it . . . I bet that's what the army did . . . Opened huge cans of store soup and you loved its old condensed-milk flavor. While I put real cream in that soup you're drinking.

ZACH. No wonder my food bills are skyrocketing . . . Cauliflower, real cream!

PETE. You told me you wanted a real cook that day . . .

ZACH. I seen you coming out of the welfare office . . . I remember.

PETE. Why don't you just say like you did to Herbie, *you took me in off the streets* . . .

ZACH. Well, what is that, taking somebody home from the welfare office if it ain't taking you off the streets.

PETE. Thanks . . . (*Takes the plate of soup and goes back with it to the kitchen*) I don't care what anybody says! That's good soup . . . God damn it!

ZACH. What's the next course?

PETE (*who has been weeping, dries his eyes with his fist and controls his sobbing*) The next course is the entree . . .

ZACH (*pretending to be cruel*). Which is?

PETE. Chicken cacciatore.

ZACH. Oh God, foreign stuff again . . . Why can't you cook American.

PETE (*brings him a plate*). Watch out, as they say in classy restaurants, a very hot plate.

ZACH. Oh, Pete, you will be the death of me . . .

PETE (*almost whispering*). Maybe you should re-enlist again . . .

ZACH. Don't you think I would if there was a real army in this country again. I'd re-enlist tonight! But there ain't no real army any more . . . The real army is . . . (*Stops as if remembering his dead buddies*)

PETE. Supposin' you eat what's put before you . . .

ZACH. I'd have a lot better appetite if you had on your chef's hat . . .

PETE. Then supposin' you go out and buy me one . . . Shell out a little money on clothing for me, since you don't pay no salary!

ZACH. You're not on the streets, are you . . . Don't you have a roof over your head and all the grub you can eat . . . And a dollar a day subway . . . Well, who do you think I am, a Rockefeller?

PETE. Why don't you shut up for a minute and eat what's put in front of you . . .

ZACH. I'll eat when I'm good and ready . . . You know what? You are one spoiled stuck-up egomaniac . . . You think anything you do is God's gift to creation . . . I'll eat this when I feel like it . . . (*Pushes his chair away from the table*)

PETE. After all the work put into that, twenty-four-hour day preparing you food, and you back away from it like that . . . You eat that! God damn you, eat that grub, when I slaved to make it.

ZACH (*shocked*). Do you realize whose house you are in.

PETE. It's my house too. You invited me to live here . . . I belong here just as much as you do . . . Don't you dare to lord it over me . . . (*Pushes Zach's chair back to the table*) Eat my food . . . I mean it, God damn it, don't you play tricks on me . . . You eat that Goddamned entree.

ZACH. Sensitive . . . All prickles . . . Can't say a thing without offending him. (*Tastes*) Hmmm . . .

PETE. Well?

ZACH. Well, Pete . . . You've outdone yourself this time . . .

PETE. You like it, Zach . . . It's . . . good?

ZACH. I said you'd outdone yourself.

PETE. Well, eat it then . . . Don't just taste it, for Christ's sake . . . Eat what I prepared for you.

ZACH. It's Italian, that's for sure . . . Very exotic . . .

PETE (*vexed, raging*). But you don't like it, is that what you mean?

ZACH. I didn't say that . . . Oh, touchy, oversensitive . . . You're a tyrant! Do you know it! You're a tyrant in my own house . . . (*Begins to eat desperately*) My God . . . My God.

PETE (*frightened*). What is it, Zach?

ZACH. Water! Water . . . Where's my glass of water?

PETE (*rushing to the sink, brings him back a glass of water*). Here.

ZACH (*drinks hurriedly*). My God, that was hot . . . Hot . . . I feel like I've swallowed a furnace . . .

PETE. But didn't you like it . . . I worked all afternoon just on that . . .

ZACH. Look inside my throat . . . Is it all blisters yet?

PETE (*goes over and sits on a stool*). Oh, my God . . . You win . . . (*Takes off his apron*) I can't please you, Zach . . . If I cut up my own hand and put it in the soup it wouldn't suit your taste buds . . . Tell you what, I'm better off on the streets . . . I'll never cook as good as your army sergeant, so why fool each other any longer.

ZACH (*apprehensive*). What else did you prepare for tonight, Pete? (*Pete stands up, folding his apron.*) I asked you a question, Pete.

PETE. I baked you a pie.

ZACH. Now you're talking . . . Pie, that's my kind of food, Pete . . . This fancy stuff with thousands of spices and condiments and everything tasting like it was something else . . . But pie!

PETE. But it's not just any kind of store pie .·. . I worked on it for two days, Zach . . . (*He begins to cry.*)

ZACH. Pete, stop it . . . Go on get me a piece of pie . . .

PETE. It's sort of special, so I guess . . .

ZACH. No, no, I'll like it. I promise to like it . . . You'll see . . . And put on your apron.

PETE. I'll get the pie, Zach. (*He folds his apron in the kitchen and puts it down on the table.*)

ZACH. All right, Petey . . . I promise I'll like it . . . I've never seen you so . . . edgy before, though. (*Said practically to himself*)

PETE (*in the kitchen, speaking also as if to himself*). I bet I spent two days on this meal . . . Reading up, shopping, making it all from scratch . . . Tasting it myself . . . It weren't no foreign meal either . . . It tasted like good homecooking to me . . . Everybody serves something foreign today anyhow . . . But this pie, God damn it, is an American pie . . . (*Coming over to Zach*) You see this pie, it's American, Zach.

ZACH. My God, it is beautiful . . .

PETE (*puts the pie down with a bang*). So you took me in off the streets, did you, huh.

ZACH. Pete, what's come over you . . . Don't you think I appreciate you . . .

PETE. Tell you what, I'm going to let you have one little bite of this and no more, on account of if you don't like it, well . . .

ZACH. But as you said, Pete . . . (*He is frightened.*) It's an American pie.

PETE. I'm going to cut you just one tiny tiny piece, 'cause if you don't like it maybe I'll send the rest to the county fair, and I bet I win the blue ribbon!

ZACH. Well, I guess I don't have no choice Pete. If you put it like that! (*Cutting him a piece, Pete holds it on a fork and extends it to Zach, who takes it in his mouth, then chews thoughtfully, finally making a face.*) Is that an American pie?

PETE (*maniacal*). Don't you know it is . . . Or has your fucking war injuries took out all your gray matter from your brain . . . Don't you know a American pie when you taste it, you motherfucker . . . Then eat it like this, hear. (*He throws the cream pie in Zach's face, then rushes to the back and gets two other pies and*

mashes these two pies all over Zach's face, chest, and hair.) There,
God damn you, now taste a real American pie all over you. I wish
you was naked so I could shove one up your ass to boot . . .
You cheap motherfucking bandit, you . . . You miserly cheap
money-grubbing cheapskate shitass! Do you think I'm going on
taking this shit from anybody. Huh? (*Zach is unable to reply be-
cause he is totally covered by lemon cream pies.*) And don't ever
come looking for me, do you hear? You stay away from me the
rest of your life, do you hear, you cheap war cripple! For the army
didn't tell you I guess when part of your brain was blowed out
they blowed out your taste buds too . . . (*He slams the door and
then one hears a terrible crash as he falls down and begins to
moan.*)

ZACH (*begins to wipe himself off from the pie*). Good God,
Jesus Christ, what has he done to me . . . I feel just like the time
the barracks blew up in . . . Where was it in . . . My God,
what have I done now . . . (*Sits brooding*) That was a bad fall
he took down the stairs all right . . . I wonder if . . . They
always told me in the army I talked too much . . . It got me
busted any number of times . . . Just about when I was to make
sergeant, I would shoot off my mouth and get busted . . . I was
lucky to get out of the army with any stripes on me, they said . . .
(*Calls*) Pete, are you all right . . . (*Goes to mirror and looks at
himself*) I look like I'd been blown up, if you ask me . . .
(*Washes himself, then comes back to chair and mopes*) Pete, I
know you're out there . . . Come on back in, why don't you,
fellow . . . I guess I drove you to it with my lip . . . Pete, I
know you're out there, and I hope you're not hurt . . . Those
stairs are treacherous all right . . . I don't want to offend you
about your cooking . . . (*Goes to the stairwell*) Are you hurt,
Pete . . . That was a nasty fall you took . . . Come on back,
Pete . . . Do you hear me, God damn you . . . I am issuing a
order . . . Get back in here. (*Pete comes slowly, shamefacedly
back, limping.*) You did hurt yourself. Take off your shoe and
sock, why don't you. (*Pete only half co-operating, Zach roughly
takes off his shoe and sock.*) You're going to have a bad bruise
there . . . (*Twists his foot*) Does that hurt? Mm . . . It does
. . . Well, you don't have no broken bones, I don't think . . .
Oh, Pete, Pete . . . What is to become of us?

PETE. You can say that! *What's to become of me* you mean.

ZACH. You have such a temper . . . I never know when it's going to explode.

PETE. No, you never play with matches, do you.

ZACH. Pete, you don't have to cook . . . Hear?

PETE. What?

ZACH. You don't have to cook . . . for me . . . You don't have to cook period.

PETE. I want to cook. You hired me for a cook and I'll cook or I'll leave.

ZACH. Cook then.

PETE. What do you mean?

ZACH. Cook anything, Pete . . . Anything . . . But don't leave . . .

PETE. God, you look awful . . . (*Goes over to the sink and brings back washcloths and basin and soap*) Here, let me clean you off . . . (*Washing him, then stops*) There's one thing I never want to hear from you again, though, whether I cook for you or not . . . Never say . . .

ZACH. Yes, Pete. Go on, my dear.

PETE. Don't call me dear . . . I'm nobody's dear. Nobody's.

ZACH. Well, tell me anyhow.

PETE. Don't never tell anybody or even breathe it to yourself you took me in off the streets . . . Or I will kill you! Do you hear? I'll cut your throat.

ZACH. I believe you would, Pete. I believe you would . . . All right, I won't ever say it again . . . In any case it ain't true.

PETE. It's true all right . . . It's the whole truth . . . But I won't hear it. I hate the truth as much as you do . . .

ZACH. What do you mean by that . . .

PETE. That . . . you can't taste anything . . . and, all right (*At a sign of rising anger*) that you ain't ever hungry anyhow on account of most of your bowels and stomach are gone . . .

ZACH. All right . . . What else . . . Go on, what else have you found out?

PETE. Ain't that enough . . .

ZACH. I'd rather have somebody say they found me on the streets than what you just said about me.

PETE. Well, forget it then, Zach, if you can . . .

ZACH. My trouble is I never forget anything . . . (*Pete rises.*) What are you doing now, for Christ's sake . . .

PETE. I thought . . . I'd take a walk around the block . . .

ZACH (*rising also*). Pete, I meant it when I said don't go . . .

PETE. I'm just going to take a walk around the block . . .

ZACH. You won't come back, Pete. I know you . . . You won't come back.

PETE. Yes, I will, Zach . . . I'll be back. (*Zach bows his head as Pete goes out.*)

ZACH (*begins to weep hard, sobs, chokes, gets up and finds Pete's apron, wipes his face with it*). (*The stage begins to grow dark.*) Well, I lost him . . . So what . . . (*Turns on the radio; it plays an old-fashioned blues number*)

(*The door opens slowly, Pete comes in, stands in the threshold . . . Zach turns down the radio . . . Pete goes over to Zach, and touches his shoulder gingerly.*)

PETE. Zach.

ZACH (*looking up*). What is it now.

PETE. I find, Zach, I guess I hurt my leg more than I thought . . .

ZACH. I was afraid . . . you had, Pete . . . Didn't I say at the time it was a bad spill you took.

PETE. Yes, I guess you did say that, come to think of it . . .

ZACH. Maybe tomorrow we should go down and have an X-ray took of it. (*He is slowly reaching for Pete's hand, but Pete puts his hand in his, and Zach throws the discarded apron around Pete.*)

PETE. Do you think a X-ray is necessary, Zach . . . I mean they are even more expensive . . . than food . . .

ZACH (*slowly taking both Pete's hands in his*). I don't care about expense no more, Pete . . . The more the expense now I think the more I will like it. (*Pulls him toward him*) Just so you stay, just so you stay.

(*Pete strokes his head.*)

THREE POEMS

BOŠKO PETROVIĆ

Translated from the Serbo-Croation by Aleksandar Nejgebauer

LULLABY

Night is a bending over yourself.
Don't you know it, man.
It's all a bit uncanny for, spread around,
the tools in your large workshop seem to be useless:
they live alone.
They know but the ways of their laws, they swerve
from the path you traced, hit sideways, keep moving
quite independently. You can't help it.
Tomorrow you will grab them again
and bring them back to the shapes, the taste, the firmness
you demand of the world. But at night
when you must be down, they do their work. (In tales
this is called: talking to each other.)
But night is a bending over yourself.
Down between a waning moon, objects and crickets,
you watch things happen as if far away.
Then you too erase yourself:
your steps fade one after another.
You see how far you got a while ago, and now
you too are gone, all by yourself, sideways.

You realize it's half as you will it, half as it will be.
And being so, you become it, too. You can't help it.
All you can do, fading one,
is to laugh a little,
laugh at yourself, bending over yourself.
And as you do, look, unexpectedly
different, in an instant you start vibrating
above the law, stronger by a smile.
And yet you sink immediately after
in their soft lap:
sleep.

DETERMINATION

On the back door red metal, moonlight sleeps.
It holds the silent glimmer of water and grass.
O sleep!
Yet I open the latticed cold and heavy
metal;
on the other side of the depths
whose nocturnal cinnabar
slowly returns to the mirror of waters,
I enter a new world
of determined darkness
where fantastic plants grow, their leaves
vaulted by stars,
while the solid forms of matter
sleep a domestic animal's sleep.

While I walk through,
neither slowly nor quickly,
surely I also leave this
moment of
lovely calm.

THE HAND

Startled in the night
by a careful hand, watchfully lowered
on my shoulders,
I leave the tumult of dreams, glassily
composed. But on the vague line of night
there remains all I left having crossed
my body's unquiet river: the battleground
still ringing with voices. Still, it is there,
that world: the late train's whistle, dripping eaves,
barking, my baggage; much more: various
forms in space. Still, not that world, mine,
the world of my knowledge, heavy with me. Now
split into separate groups, a herd
of animals, whose movements are quite
unfamiliar, their breath is cold. I know
only the one I was startled by,
with the noisy fair across
the river. The one I am not. I not I,
glassily composed, pure, undisturbed. Myself
a whole, unintelligible too, finally
unaware of my next move's power and path.
And yet, full of some great and easy knowledge!
What a hand, carefully lowered
on my shoulders.

NOTES ON CONTRIBUTORS

HOMERO ARIDJIS was born in Mexico in 1940 and has been his country's ambassador to Switzerland and the Netherlands. His book *Mirándola dormir* won the Xavier Villaurrutia Prize for the best book of 1964, and he was awarded Guggenheim Fellowships in 1966 and 1979. A collection of his poems in English translation, *Blue Spaces*, was published by Seabury Press in 1975, and *Exaltation of Light*, from which these poems are taken, is available from Boa Editions. For information on ELIOT WEINBERGER, see the note below on page 186.

EDWIN BROCK is poetry editor of the English literary magazine *Ambit*, and his poems have appeared in such American magazines as *The New Yorker, Antaeus*, and *Partisan Review*. New Directions has published his satirical *Paroxisms* (1974), an autobiographical work, *Here. Now. Always.* (1977), and four books of poetry, most recently *The River and the Train*, in 1979.

A native of Portugal, MARIO CESARINY has been associated with the Surrealist movement that started there in the late 1940s. He has published essays on various subjects and earns his living mainly through the sale of his oils and collages. JONATHAN GRIFFIN has translated Fernando Pessoa's *Collected Poems* (Penguin, 1974) and Jorge De Sena's *Sobre Esta Praia: Eight Meditations on the Coast of the Pacific* (Mudborn, 1979). JEAN R. LONGLAND, Curator of the Library of the Hispanic Society of New York, received the Portugal Prize from the International Poetry Association and the Portuguese government in 1973.

ANTONIO CISNEROS was born in 1942 in Peru. He won that country's National Poetry Prize in 1965, first prize for poetry in the Casa de las Américas competition (Havana) in 1968, and a Guggenheim Fellowship in 1978. He has taught at English, French, and Hungarian universities and is presently at the University of San Marcos in Lima. A collection of his poems through 1969, *The Spider Hangs Too Far from the Ground*, was published by Cape/ Grossman in 1970. MAUREEN AHERN, a professor of Latin American literature at Arizona State University, was educated in Peru, where she co-edited *Havarec*, a bilingual literary magazine. She edited the anthology *Peru: The New Poetry* (Red Dust, 1977) with the English poet and translator DAVID TIPTON. WILLIAM ROWE teaches Latin American Literature at Kings College, London, and is co-editor of *Ecuatorial*, a bilingual magazine of Latin American poetry.

RUTH DOMINO's native language is German, but after she emigrated to the U.S. during W. W. II her English language fiction was published in *The New Yorker* and *The Kenyon Review*. The poems here are translated from the Italian, the language of her present home. DANIEL HOFFMAN has been a consultant in poetry of the Library of Congress and is presently Poet in Residence at the University of Pennsylvania. He has written *Brotherly Love, The Center of Attention*, and other books of verse. Author of *Mount Allegro, A Passion for Sicilians, Reunion in Sicily*, and other books, JERRE MANGIONE organized the Center for Italian Studies at the University of Pennsylvania.

A professor of English at California State University in San Francisco, ROBIN GAJDUSEK has written *Hemingway's Paris* (Scribner's, 1978) and *The King, The Queen, and The Celluloid Throne*, a study of contemporary film. This is the first publication of his poetry.

Born of peasant stock in Carnac in 1907, GUILLEVIC is one of the most highly regarded of living French poets. A bilingual edition of his *Selected Poems*, translated by Denise Levertov, was published by New Directions in 1969, and his work has also appeared in *ND34*. DORI KATZ is a professor of Modern Languages and Literatures at Trinity College and has translated Marguerite Yourcenar's *Fires* (Farrar, Straus and Giroux, 1981).

RUSSELL HALEY, whose work also appeared in *ND42*, lives in New Zealand, where his first collection of stories, *The Sauna Bath Mysteries*, came out in 1978. Earlier publications, of poetry, were *The Walled Garden* (1972) and *On the Fault Line* (1977). He is now working on *Northern Lights*, an extended but discontinuous narrative.

Born in Schwerte, West Germany, in 1942, RÜDIGER KREMER studied German literature, art history, and journalism at the universities of Münster and Bremen. From 1968 to 1972 he was an editor at Radio Bremen. He is now a free-lance writer in that city and has just published *Donald-Donald,* a new volume of poems. BREON MITCHELL, whose translations of Kremer's work have also appeared in *ND27, ND33,* and *ND41,* is a professor of German and Comparative Literature at Indiana University. His *James Joyce and the German Novel* was published in 1976 by Ohio University Press.

LAWRENCE MILLMAN has written stories, poems, translations, and *Our Like Will Not Be There Again* (Little, Brown), about the last of the Irish storytellers and their tales, which was nominated for the Pulitzer Prize in 1977. A long-time collector of folktales, he draws on their spirit in "Origins," part of his larger *Book of Origins.*

Author of *The Autobiography of Cassandra: Princess and Prophetess of Troy* (Archer Editions, 1979), *Bastards: Footnotes to History* (Treacle, 1979), and *Encores for a Dilettante* (Fiction Collective, 1978), URSULE MOLINARO lives in New York City.

ALAIN NADAUD's first volume of stories, from which this interview is taken, appeared in 1980 under the title of *La Tache aveugle* in Paris. Nadaud has also published translations of the fiction of the Indian writer Vilas Sarang, one of whose stories, translated by Breon Mitchell, appeared in *ND41.* This is Nadaud's first appearance in English. For information on BREON MITCHELL, see the note above, page 184, on Rüdiger Kremer.

Biographical information on ANTÓNIO OSÓRIO is given in the translator's introduction. GIOVANNI PONTIERO teaches in the department of Spanish and Portuguese Studies at the University of Manchester. He has published translations and anthologies of various Brazilian and Portuguese writers; his translations have appeared in *ND37* and *ND39.*

For information on JUSTO JORGE PADRÓN see the translator's introduction. LOUIS BOURNE's book of poems *Médula de la llama* won second prize in the recent Gules competition (all the other applicants were Spaniards). Bourne is an American who lives in Madrid, where his translations of Vicente Aleixandre and others have been published.

BOŠKO PETROVIĆ was born in Romania in 1915, and he now lives and works in Novi Sad, Yugoslavia. He has published novels and several collections of poems and short stories. The present selection was translated from the Serbo-Croatian by ALEKSANDAR NEJGE-

BAUER, born in 1930, who also lives in Novi Sad, and has published two collections of his own verse.

Since his first collection of fiction, *Color of Darkness* (New Directions, 1957), JAMES PURDY has been a strong presence on the literary scene. Arbor House has published his recent novels: *In a Shallow Grave* (1976), *Narrow Rooms* (1978), and *The Mourners Below* (1980).

GIOVANNI RABONI has published many books in Italy and is an editor at the Mondadori Publishing House in Milan. VINIO ROSSI teaches French and Italian at Oberlin College. He has translated the work of Eugenio Montale and written the introduction to Montale's *The Storm*, published by Field/Oberlin. STUART FRIEBERT directs the writing program at Oberlin and co-edits *Field*. He has published nine books of original verse in English and German as well as translations from many languages.

MICHAEL RECK is a professor of English at the University of Puerto Rico. He is the author of the widely acclaimed *Ezra Pound: A Close-up* (McGraw-Hill, 1967), and his poetry has appeared in earlier ND anthologies and numerous literary magazines.

Fiction and criticism by JOAN RETALLACK have appeared in the U.S. and abroad in such publications as *Ambit, Epoch,* and *A Critical Assembling* (Assembling Press). Retallack is a lecturer in the General Honors Program at the University of Maryland and a member of the Forum on Psychiatry and the Humanities at the Washington School of Psychiatry.

A native of San Antonio, GEOFFREY RIPS won a CAPS grant for fiction in 1979. He is currently co-ordinator of the Freedom to Write program at PEN American Center.

ANNE WALDMAN is the author of *Journals & Dreams,* co-editor of *Talking Poetics* (Annals of the Jack Kerouac School of Disembodied Poetics, vols. 1 & 2), and co-editor of *Rocky Ledge* magazine.

ELIOT WEINBERGER lives in New York City and is the editor and publisher of *Montemora*. He has translated *Eagle or Sun?* and *A Draft of Shadows and Other Poems* by Octavio Paz, both published by New Directions.